THE MONSTER I LOVE

THE
MONSTER
I LOVE

ISBN: 978-1-962665-01-8

THE
MONSTER
I LOVE

AUTHORS

YD LA MAR

S.L. SINCLAIR

STEPHANIE ELLIS

K.C. BORDERS

STEFANIE DAWN

SERENA MOSSGRAVES

RAYNE MATTHEWS

EDITOR

LILY LUCHESI

ARTIST

BLUE RAVEN BOOK COVERS

INTRODUCTION

Two inherent emotions within the human psyche are fear and lust. While everyone experiences them differently, they exist, and oftentimes, they exist in tandem.

Why else do film directors ensure those killed off by the villain are the amorous ones? Why else does love save the day when the bad guy is moments away from victory?

Before the term "fangirl" was coined, Count Dracula — ghoulish visage and all — was noted for having the most ardent female admirers, both within fiction and real life, at the movies. Before most of us knew what lust and love even were, we were blushing as inhuman, somehow phallic, appendages held our favorite anime characters bound against their will.

What is it about monsters, ones who can't even pretend to be human, that attracts so many of us, whether or not we want to acknowledge the feeling? The mystery? The danger? The sheer, inhuman violence?

Some combination of it all?

Perhaps we will never know.

The human mind and body are strange things, and the body wants what it wants, sometimes without the mind's consent.

Here in this anthology, you will find less love, more lust, and certainly more blood as some of the best talents in horror and dark romance today bring you their interpretations of Lovecraftian horrors.

Sit down, relax with your chosen beverage, and let Fractured Mind Publishing bring you new horrors and desires, the likes of which you can only imagine in your nightmares.

— USA Today bestselling author Lily Luchesi, FMP acquisitions editor

THE PRICE OF SHADOWS

YD LA MAR

CHAPTER ONE

The branch whips my face, lancing my skin, and I welcome the sharp pain.. As the cold temperature continues to seep through the layers of my clothes, thoughts of my sister's possible murder move me forward.

This forest is alive with haunting whispers on the wind. The multitude of shadowed branches reach out like accusing fingers to brush against my skin, calling me deeper into the depths of its maw.

The crunch of leaves beneath my boot is a welcome distraction from the gnawing ache of uncertainty. I look around the darkness, interspersed with minimal lunar illumination reminiscent of silver tendrils of an otherworldly plane. It beckons with the temptation of possible answers to the questions I have. The authorities may have labeled her disappearance as a simple case of a missing person; I know better.

The officers said the crime scene didn't have any evidence of her survival. Splatters of blood were left behind in a secluded location of the forest, with signs of cult rituals and animal bones scattered about. The memory of the torches lingers in my mind, the flicking flames mimicking a seductive siren's dance to the evil entities my sister used to play with. It was by luck that her weird get-togethers with her 'friends' never ended with the forest being struck down in flames.

A twig snaps beneath my shoe and my eyes widen, unsure if there are any beasts hidden behind the shadows.

"There's no other way. I'm the only person who can find her," I remind myself, the weight of responsibility heavy on my shoulders. Our town and family have long since given up the search, but they didn't know my sister like I did. She was a fighter, not one to simply vanish into the night without a struggle.

"Hold on, Sarai," I whisper to the trees, watching their leaves sway beneath the influence of a chilling breeze that promises of something foreboding—a presence lurking in the shadows, watching and waiting.

I've come too far to turn back now. Forcing myself to swallow my growing dread, I pull my sweater tighter to my chest and push deeper into the heart of the forest.

Somewhere in these haunted woods lies the truth and it's up to me to find it and bring her back.

I push deeper into the forest, the shadows of the branches twist and contort, taking on a life of their own while the moonlight wanes from the cover of clouds. *How long have I been out here?* My breaths turn into visible puffs in front of me. Each step I take into the unknown has me thinking my mind is playing tricks on me, telling me I'm descending into madness.

Spontaneously taking a turn in a new direction, I shiver and look at my surroundings, the air thick with the stench of decay and despair.

"Sarai, your friends would choose a place like this for another ritual. Maybe I'm getting close."

Wondering if talking to myself is the first sign of losing my mind in this labyrinth of trees and boulders, I tilt my head to the sky and send out a mental prayer to whatever higher power is watching over me—perhaps shaking their head at the stupidity of my decisions.

A howl rents the air from a great distance and a chill goes down my spine. Whipping my head around, I look behind me, uncertain if I hear the rustling of forest creatures or something far more sinister.

Just keep moving. Don't stand still!

I run, hoping the position of the moon will guide me in the right direction. I can't shake the feeling I'm being followed even if my eyes tell me there's nothing there but the oppressive silence of the night. But the eerie silence brings with it paranoia. *It's not normal for it to be this quiet here, is it? No sound of insects or birds taking flight from my presence?*

This is how horror movies start, Jenny, I remind myself, much to the chagrin of my spiraling thoughts. My mind races with terrifying possibilities, but I keep going for my sister's sake. I will not become another victim in this twisted tale of horror.

I stumble upon an unexpected clearing. *Why would something like this be here? It wasn't here before…*

Another tentative step, and my pulse throbs behind my ears as my breathing escalates from alarm. Before my eyes, a short distance away, is a scene straight out of my own worst nightmares. The ground is littered with bones, their bleached white surfaces gleaming in the moonlight like macabre decorations. Faint laughter resounds around me and my body tenses.

I'm unsure of what's real and what's not, wondering when the last time I took a sip of water. Perhaps dehydration is kicking in and I'm beginning to show signs of hallucinations. Something crawls along my skin like phantom fingers caressing my flesh with the promise of malevolence.

· · ·

My frigid breath sputters and I startle back, the hairs on the back of my neck standing on end. With a gasp, I stumble and fall, my hands and feet scrambling desperately on the forest floor, trying to put distance between myself and whatever unseen horror lurks in the darkness.

But there's nothing there. Not in front of me, not beside me.

"You're losing your mind, Jenny. Get up. Stop acting like this," I whisper, trying to encourage myself out loud. *I need to find Sarai. What if she's caught in whatever this is? Who else will bring her back?*

Panic claws at my chest, threatening to overwhelm me as I struggle to regain my footing. Every instinct screams at me to run, but I chose instead to force myself to stay in position.

Creeping forward behind one of the tree trunks before the clearing, I peek around, observing how the forest seems to stretch forever in every direction around it. Everything looks the same. *Anyone can easily get lost here. If Sarai is lost, how long has she been without food and water? By the time I realized she was gone, days could have passed.*

My heart continues to pound in my chest, the sound of its frantic rhythm drowning out all other noise and in a way, helping to push some of my fears aside. *Is this what they mean by adrenaline leading you?*

Crossing the clearing would be the fastest way to

the other side. Going the roundabout way increases the chances of getting lost, the entire forest a mirror of itself like a taunting maze of trees.

With an audible gulp and a burst of false courage, I make the spontaneous decision to cross the clearing. Adrenaline surges through my veins as I propel myself forward, sprinting as fast as my legs can carry me without looking back

Bones crunch beneath my feet, sending a shiver down my spine, but I force myself to ignore the sickening sound. My focus is singular—reach the other side of the clearing, find any sign of my sister, and get out of this nightmare forest with her in tow, even if it means I have to carry her on my back.

Moving shadows dance at the edges of my vision, taunting me with their shifting forms, but I convince myself it's the clouds above teasing the moon's glow again.

Sweat trickles down my back, mingling with the chill of the night air and I feel a cramp set into my calf at the most inopportune moment.

No! Not now! Keep going!

But the path in front of me wavers, the shimmer of air reminding me of the heat in a scorching desert. I rub my eyes, trying to dispel the hallucination but when my vision clears, I'm no longer in the clearing. I jolt in a panic, the terror of what's happening to me squeezing the air from my lungs. The forest vanishes, replaced by the oppressive darkness of a dank, foreboding cave. I crouch in fear, my instincts forcing me to make myself small in order to feel less vulnerable.

The walls threaten to close around me, dripping with moisture and slick from unrecognizable sources. The shadows, once dancing between the branches, follow me here, mocking in metaphorical laughter between the mysterious glow from the walls.

"Where am I?" I dare whisper to myself, wincing when my voice echoes against the stone walls.

The air here is thick with the musty smell of decay. With trembling hands, I rise to my feet, pulling my sweater around me as if it will offer some semblance of false protection. I sweep my gaze around me, and find nothing but darkness in every direction; a cave that forces you to choose a path that might lead to death.

Realization hits: the only choice that presents itself is to stay here and die where I stand or choose one of the tunnels. *Maybe Sarai fell upon the same weird portal I just fell through? There were ritualistic bones in the clearing. It's a high probability, right?*

When a rock skids across my feet, I scream in terror, sprinting toward the closest tunnel to get away from whatever caused it. My heart wants to leap out of my throat during my race deeper in my chosen direction, the walls closing in on me. My rapid footsteps echo off the damp stone, the sound reverberating ominously, creating the illusion of something else giving me chase.

There's a mysterious glow that pulses from the walls, dimly illuminating my steps when I step into a larger chamber. I accidentally kick a loose pebble and a cacophony of rapid fluttering fills the air. A swarm of bats bursts forth from the darkness, their wings beating furiously as they swoop and dive around me in a frenzy. I scream in horror, slapping my head and trying to cover it at the same time, stumbling backward in a blind panic.

My feet carry me back the way I came with reckless abandon. The walls of the tunnel blur past me while I run with no actual idea of where I'm going. When I find myself back to where I think I started, I collapse to the ground, gasping for air.

Tears prick my eyes as I struggle to catch my breath, the terror of the encounter still fresh in my mind. *Do bats eat human flesh?* I peek around my feet, expecting to see a scattering of human bones but there's nothing of the sort, simply dirt and loose rock.

I bring my knees up and bury my face, attempting to bring calm to my system by rocking myself.

"Sarai, where are you?" I sob against my arms, hopelessness threatening to drown me.

CHAPTER TWO

The cave is reminiscent of the belly of a beast, life pulsing through the glow of its rocks, exhaling dampness. The worst part is the feeling that the cavern walls are closing in like ribs. Wishing I had a lantern, I grab a nearby rock the size of my palm and begin to desperately chip away at the wall in hopes of revealing more of the mysterious illumination.

Perhaps, if I break away enough, the glow will be brighter, enough to cast away some of the darkness that surrounds me.

Panting from exertion, the sound loud in my ears, my eyes occasionally flick to the ceiling full of stalactites, reminding me of sharp teeth waiting to bite down on my flesh when I least expect it. A sudden flutter of wings and scattering of pebbles sends a ripple through my spine; I can't help but warily turn to look behind me. My mind urges caution, warning against it, but the pull is irresistible, influenced by an unknown spell cast over me.

There it stands—a creature of nightmares—before me. A being seemingly to have been made from the depths of Hell with its obsidian color. The longer I stare, the more I notice its smooth, oily, whale-like surface—not at all what one would think of when lost in a cave. The creature's terrifying, deadly horns curve inward toward each other, adding to its twisted form. Bat-like wings beat silently behind it, an eerie phenomenon my mind is currently unable to wrap around. It hovers a foot off the cavern ground, mocking my inability to find my way out of here. Grotesque prehensile paws and a barbed tail only amplify the dread I feel coursing through me.

But what chills me to the bone is the frightening blankness where a face should be, a void that recon-firms my suspicions that this thing originates from the belly of Hell itself.

Memories of my sister and her choice of reading material flit through my mind at that very moment. She adored Lovecraft's storytelling and I remember her mentioning a bat-like creature a time or two.

A night-gaunt—a Lovecraftian monster devoid of speech, laughter, or smiles judging by its faceless presentation. The being's only capabilities according to what I'm witnessing are clutching, flying, and instilling fear, which it's doing a great job of.

But the logical part of my mind refuses to believe in the impossible, unfiltering my mouth probably to my own demise.

"Why are you here?" I blurt out, my voice trembling.

The night-gaunt's laughter booms from the pit of an abyss, unseen, an unnerving cacophony of forgotten screams most likely from damned souls.

Is Sarai one of them?

"Seeker of forbidden truths," it hisses from who knows where, "you tread where sanity unravels. What knowledge do you seek?"

My heart threatens to explode out of my chest from its demonic, preternatural multivoice. I press my back against the wall where my previous chipping occurred and shut my eyes, forcing myself to think logically. *If it wants me dead, I would already be dead. But I'm not. It's talking to me. I'm the only one here.*

What's the question? What am I looking for? Knowledge I'm seeking?

"I-I seek my sister. Blood of my blood. Sarai."

"What price do you pay?" it demands with authority, not once hinting to any possible answers he may have pertinent to what I'm rambling.

Desperation claws at my chest, the emotion wanting to manifest itself into physicality, to rip my flesh from bone. Memories of my sister and her smiles, of our shared moments, run through my mind like an uncontrollable stream of consciousness. *Is this what they mean when they say life passes before your eyes when you're face to face with death?*

The night-gaunt's laughter echoes through the cave before he dips his head frighteningly toward me. "A memory," it whispers menacingly. "A cherished memory, willingly surrendered. Do you truly believe that will be enough of a sacrifice?"

I whimper at its proximity, my forehead perspiring profusely despite the chill that bites the air in this mysterious cavern of hell.

"Your fear is exquisite," it says and my mind supplies the image of a wicked tongue licking across his nonexistent lips.

"I-I don't know what price is expected of me," I admit, my voice shaking.

Something undulates beneath his skin reminiscent of maggots crawling under the surface of his flesh. I blink a few times, unsure if my mind is playing tricks on me in this dim light. *It could just be his veins... veins that move.*

The creature leans closer, his skin smelling of brimstone and sulfur. "Truths buried deep fester. The more you try to hide, the more I see behind the facade—deeper into your debauched nature."

My mind races. *What is it talking about? What is it implying?*

"Man fools himself into thinking control is all it takes. Do you wish to reveal your true power, mortal? Your true… nature in sin?"

Is he still speaking of secrets? Sin? Like things I've done wrong? People I've wronged? I have plenty. Everyone does. The forbidden love I've hidden, the betrayal I've witnessed, the fact that I let my sister get this far with her friend group and their rituals. But there's one darker gnawing truth I've entombed deep in my subconscious; the night-gaunt can't possibly be aware of it.

"Power? No. I'm just here for my sister. Where is she?" I try again.

Enraged by my lack of understanding, the night-gaunt's non-face darkens in fury as it seizes me with its twisted claws. With a deafening roar, it drags me through another shimmering wave in the atmosphere and into the depths of what feels like the abyss of *Dante's Inferno*. My screams echo through the infernal abyss until they become drowned out by the moans and cries of agony that surround us.

"Mercy!" I cry out, my voice drowned by the cacophony of torment that surrounds me. But there is no reprieve, no solace in this realm of eternal suffering. Fires lick my flesh, singing the hairs along my arms and part of my head. No amount of tears can cool my face as we delve deeper and deeper into this living nightmare.

The flames threaten to consume me. I realize too late the folly of my sins, the weight of my secrets now laid bare in the inferno's merciless embrace. Is this what the night-gaunt wanted of me? For me to confess all that's scarred my soul in its dark taint?

"I'll tell you my secrets! Please, have mercy!"

Haunting moans lift in the air as the flames come to life like a living being, stretching itself toward me. The hairs of my nares singe off completely, the smell of human fat burning, melting into a sizzle while I claw at my face with my nails, trying to rid myself of the agonizing pain.

The night-gaunt's faceless head morphs back and forth, the image wavering either from the heat or my mind attempting to piece together what's left of my sanity.

"What price do you pay, human?" he demands as the bones of my fingers become visible, blackened by the living flames.

With a final breath from my charred lungs, I cough out, "Whatever pleases you."

He shoves his non-face against mine, his wings expanding to formidable levels before he beats them one more time, lifting us from the flames. Did I think I would get a reprieve? I can feel my flesh knitting itself back, inch by sickening inch. It feels like a million insects burying themselves between my muscles. In my weakness, I'm unable to fight it off, forced to submit to their tortures as tendons reattach themselves to bone.

My body is tossed against jagged rocks, their sharp edges piercing my back upon the fall. Movement catches my eyes and I watch with fright as ghastly figures pull themselves from a river of lava, crawling on hands to expose the lower parts of their torsos ripped off. I want to gag at the smell of their innards being dragged across the dusty ground but my throat muscles haven't yet regenerated enough to allow me to. One of them shoots out a half-melted arm and grabs onto my leg. My reknit flesh sizzles from the contact. Tears prick my eyes and I sob through the burning smoke wafting in my direction, wondering how long I will be forced to experience this hell.

An eerie chuckle cuts through the cries of men torn in pieces, mindlessly crawling around the area.

"In the realm beyond, behold how effortlessly mortals surrender to their vices. Their follies, like shimmering veils, cloak them, and temptations weave their inevitable descent." He punctuates the last word but I can't pay him any mind at the moment.

The half-dead man continues to pull at my leg and I struggle to kick him off. When my other foot lands on his skull, cracking his neck, he cries in mock pain and proceeds to dig his nails into my calf, embedding them.

"I don't understand your riddles! I told you I'll pay your price!" I scream, unsure if my body will go into shock or if that mercy's been taken from me too, in this place.

The night-gaunt crushes the man's skull in, his brain matter splattering to the side of his inhuman feet, bent backward as if to remind me I'm no longer on the mortal plane. The smell of rotting corpses rises with the billowing heat and I realize my nares have regained their senses, much to my dismay.

The man's blood begins to coagulate, then bubble, morphing into little demons that jump into the next crawling half-torso. The man opens his mouth to scream, only to have one of the little demons pull out his tongue with a splash of crimson, and then jump down his throat to choke him.

This is it. My request will go unheard and I will die here among the tainted.

Just as I begin to close my eyes, welcoming death, slick obsidian claws expand from their original form, piercing my abdomen before taking us both aflight.

CHAPTER THREE

I stumble backward, my breath hitching in the frigid night air. The once-dappled moon now bears witness to my trembling, naked form out in the open. Falling to my knees, my hands roam my bloodstained skin to find no evidence of any recent open wounds.

How is this possible?

The malevolent creature before me takes a step forward, eclipsing the remaining light of the moon behind him.

"Mortal," it hisses, elongating the syllables into a macabre melody. His faceless features stare down at me like hell's sentinel. "You seek power, do you not?"

"I-I seek to find my sister," I insist, my voice a mere whisper, my body threatening to collapse from all it's been put through. Or perhaps it's another trick of the mind. My muscles have evidently returned to their original state, but something tells me my body won't be able to take what I'm asking for.

"You seek what you already know."

I whip my head toward him, shaking on my knees. "I—I want to escape this wretched hell. Have we returned to Earth? Are we back in the mortal plane? Is my punishment over?" I ramble.

It's the wrong thing to ask but it slips my lips anyway. The creature's laughter rebounds through the trees, a dissonant sound of madness and screeches threatening to burst my eardrums.

"Ah, sweet Mortal," it croons, sending a shiver down my spine. "Power demands sacrifice. Your fear, your very essence—it shall deliciously sustain my hunger for tonight."

My terror intensifies. I glimpse something of my own reflection in the moon's glow across the slick skin of the night-gaunt's back—a reflection that's twisted, and hollow.

"What is my price?" I ask again, afraid to hear the answer.

"Your memories will serve for what I have in store for us," it murmurs, visible tendrils of darkness reaching for my mind. The night-gaunt's claws throw me back against the ground, his weight holding me down in a vulnerable position.

The barbed tail wraps itself around my thigh, digging into my flesh as it pulls my legs apart. The monster extrudes a horrendous phallic organ that twists until it shapes itself into a head with teeth, then pulses with clawed serpents beneath the flesh, their sharp talons making their way through the barrier now and again, piercing the flesh of his shaft.

Before I can fight him off, he enters me in one heartrending thrust, cutting my insides along the way. I cry but no sound escapes as he rips the flesh of his face and forces a long, sinewy black tongue down my throat to swallow my screams.

His next thrust brings forth memories dancing before me—the warmth of an embrace, the taste of forbidden kisses.

The night hangs heavy, a shroud of wickedness drapes over my exposed skin. His barbed tail pulls me wider, forcing me to make way for his invasion as his phallic member continues to shred me from the inside. What I don't account for is another prehensile organ protruding from between his legs, entering my nether regions, stretching me beyond human capabilities.

I cry into his ripped mouth and he bites down on my tongue, not fully tearing it apart, to silence my screams, choking me with my blood.

My heart pounds in sync with the howling of the wind, visions of the past pulling me away from the present.

Transported, I stand there, watching my sister and her husband in spite, scratching the length of my arms until warm blood drips onto the floor. They say covetousness is like a doorway to darkness, a threshold crossed with eyes shut. Once opened, it gnaws at your soul, insatiable. The taint seeps, relentless, toward your heart, staining every beat with resentment.

The creature thrusts into my body harder, dragging me across the clearing atop the scattered bones, the air around him aflame with hunger. Each of his harsh movements pull me in and out of the past.

"Mortal Jenny," it hisses, its voice a serrated blade. "Why cling to your fragile humanity? Embrace the abyss within."

My breath catches at his use of my name. I never gave it to him. "What do you want from me? I'm innocent," I sob, unable to do much more than continue to accept his assault. The worst part of it is, my skin pebbles with goosebumps, challenging my conscious mind over the fact that I'm not actively fighting him off, despite having the physical capabilities.

"Innocence? A fragile illusion, woven from threads of denial. Beneath your skin, darkness pulses, a dormant tempest," it croons like a nefarious lover.

He flips me over and expands his wings as if prepared for battle, right before he enters my ass with his serrated cock that pulses. The other protrusion works together with his barbed tail, prodding my entrance once again.

.   .   .

"I—I am not like you," I cry out with conviction, this new position giving me slight reprieve without his tongue diving down my throat. I cough and sputter out blood onto the grass, clawing on the ground to get away from the night-gaunt to no avail.

"Yet," it whispers against my ear, "you hunger for release. Why deny your true nature? Unify with me, and taste eternity."

His thrusts drag my face along the loose pebbles, a human skull a scant few feet away facing me, mocking me with a stupid, macabre grin. The fraying edges of my memories call out like a siren. Laughter, love, all fading, transforming into me... on my back accepting my sister's husband into my womb with debauched desperation. He fucks me deliciously, the way I always imagined and I embolden him to desecrate my flesh to his desires, whispering encouragements in his ear. The only problem is, once it slips my lips, he rears back as if possessed, dislodging himself and stumbling to the farthest wall with a stricken look of betrayal across his features.

"Who are you?" he seethes, his eyes full of accusation.

"What do you mean?" I feign hurt innocence, knowing full well my sister and I share the same face and body.

It's unfair for her not to share his flesh with me! We are one and the same, blood of my blood. Can't he see how I welcome him into my body? The way we fit perfectly.

"Get out! Get out of my sight! What the hell is wrong with you?" The rejection tears into a part of me I never wished to see, releasing a heinous darkness that's grown over the span of my covetousness. My heart shatters before the man I gave my virginity to, the only person capable of rendering me paralyzed in the moment. Something monstrous inside my heart begins to bleed. The ritualistic chants play through my mind like a broken record and I curse myself for not doing it again before we arrived here. I needed them stronger, I needed him to hunger for me the way I hungered for him!

"Why?" I cry out into the night, my sobs wracking my body with shudders. The night-gaunt's cock worms its way beyond my womb, attempting to fill the void *he* left behind.

"Do you feel how well your body welcomes me? The way it parts for me to tear your insides asunder. You feel so good wrapped around me, Jenny. I want to bury myself deeper inside your fleshly vessel, to make us one the way you've always craved it."

"Lies! All of it is lies! I did what I had to do. He belonged to me!" I scream wildly.

The night-gaunt turns me to my side, holding one of my legs up against his shoulder as his barbed tail wriggles its way between the apex of my legs, uncaring of the searing fresh wounds it shreds crosses once more. My hand shoots to my stomach, trying to push it down, my skin slick with sweat. The night grows colder and more ominous, the forest around us silent as death itself.

"Your pebbled skin dances along the shadows, where sins birth galaxies. Embrace it, Jenny. Become the void, for I promise to embed myself into your very existence the way you begged me to." He groans when his cock pulses, but doesn't stop thrusting, choosing instead to rip a hole into my abdomen with his claws and lean down to drink from my life essence.

As the stars begin to blink out from my vision, I hesitate to say any more. The abyss beckons an invitation to oblivion.

"What price do you pay, Jenny, to have me bury my spawn in your womb, to offer such delicious crimson lifeblood into my being, tempting me with your decadent sins?"

"I offer you nothing!" I scream, my eyes fluttering as his teeth bite down and tear a chunk out of my stomach and intestines.

The wet sounds of his chewing and his groans on the verge of ecstasy play again and again, drowning out the screams of the dead that call me back to the hellscape we came from.

"You offer me *everything…*"

"The universe thrives on chaos. Your sins—the sweet nectar of existence. Feed them to me, and ascend."

My pulse quickens despite my eyes telling me I'm actively dying. He continues to feast on my flesh, pounding his cock and tail inside of me with no mercy. I watch with morbid fascination as his long black tongue licks up my wound, trailing blood to my breast right before he bites down around my nipple.

Self-hatred pours itself into my veins like liquid hot magma as I find pleasure in his torture, a moan slipping through my lips.

Flickers of his stricken face. Flickers of her smeared mascara and hostility and resentment. Flickers of her body tied to the ground as my blade plunged into her chest cavity with an audible crack, tears streaming down my face through gritted teeth.

I close my eyes and feel my memories unravel like a spider's fragile silk.

The way he begged. The way my pulse quickened, having him at my mercy. The way his eyes dilated right before I carved out his heart and took a loving bite to dedicate my love to him, to show him he belonged to me.

The night carried with it my sorrow while I spilled tears over his corpse, offering her to the darkness in replacement for what was taken from me.

The night-gaunt's claws against my cheek, ripping my flesh, bring me back to the present as he slithers his thick tongue down my throat again. I sigh, my body responding to my subconscious desires despite how my logical mind continues to fight and change the narrative of truth.

How can I admit the creature is right? My legs slowly wrap themselves around his grotesque form, welcoming the way he tears me apart above the ritual site, our bodies moving in a dance as old as time.

The choice looms—an eternity of living in falsehood, the lies I've carefully woven to meticulously become Jenny... or the seductive abyss he offers, tempting the true monster that dwells inside.

"And if I refuse?" I pant, my hands digging holes into

the night-gaunt's neck, basking in the way his black blood tricks down my arm, tickling my sensitive skin, a trail of running mascara reminding me of her patheticness.

The creature grins through its torn facial flesh, teeth like shards of broken promises. "Then wander lost, forever yearning. But remember, *Sarai*: darkness is patient, and any possibility of redemption fades like forgotten stars."

And so, beneath the moon's indifferent gaze, I surrender. My sins dance a wicked waltz while our bodies collide, slipping against our combined blood while he continues to feast on my flesh—moaning a symphony of damnation that echoes through eternity.

His wings tremble right before I'm thrown over the decadent precipice of the impossible. My scream reverberates between the trees, then swallowed by darkness. I struggle, riding the waves of pain and pleasure, futile against the night-gaunt's power over me. Trepidation and anticipation both claw at my chest, my memories muddled and disrupted by our vile tryst.

The night-gaunt releases his own finish inside my growing corpse, then takes another loving bite, licking the edges of my exposed rib cage beneath the beating of my heart. I finally understand— This is the trade made that fateful night. Both sisters lost to shadows, both bound by sacrifice.

His groans play on as he finishes inside of me again, his release seeping through my wound, mixed with blood and dark tendrils that transform into demon maggots. But I no longer feel anything while I silently watch his body dance against mine toward oblivion.

In the depths of the forest, my sacrifice is but a fleeting moment, a single note in the symphony of suffering that plagues my mind. None of us are innocent here, no matter how much we try to convince ourselves otherwise. Reasons and justifications die slow deaths, the unavoidable fate we seal ourselves in once we trespass. Darkness is like a taint, continuing to stain us from within out of mortal sight. And what is mortality? Sacrificial vessels made of carbon. From the dust we came, to the dust we must be given to. The night-gaunt feeds on souls, its hunger insatiable. I have delved too deeply into the darkness, and now my fate is sealed with his like a lover's depraved embrace.

My eyelids flutter as I go in and out of consciousness, and beneath the calm of the chilling night air, the monster grabs the organ beneath my ribs and squeezes, jerking me awake. Gasping for breath, straining with the remnants of my life, I wonder if I will go out with one final exquisite torture.

The forest around me whispers ancient laments; the cries of others who have danced with the night-gaunt, their memories lost, their existence reduced to spectral echoes. I'll join their ranks, my soul to be condemned to wander the shadows for all eternity. If I'm lucky, maybe I'll get to play with those I visited down in Hell.

But my eyes widen when the image of the night-gaunt shimmers, morphing into my sister's face. Jenny stares down at me with a wicked smile, wrinkling her nose in distaste.

"You never could be yourself. Always wanting to be exactly like me. Always wanting what belongs to me. Being my twin doesn't mean we are the same person, Sarai."

I growl, my hands going around her neck, my fingers slipping across black blood belonging to the night-gaunt.

A snarl rumbles beneath his skin, a warning that it's not over.

His face shimmers once more and I unexpectedly feel the heat of flames closing in. Living fire that chuckles with chitter-chatters of little demons, beckoning me to return. The cries of the tortured call me by name, my ears keen on the way it caresses me, as if it's me who forgot where home is all this time.

The night-gaunt squeezes my organ again, jerking his fist up, cracking my ribs in the process. Choking on blood, I tell myself it's probably better to drown in my life force than to welcome death through the melting of my flesh from eternal flames.

The echoes of my despair fade into the abyss that dance along the edges of my vision. The forest suddenly lights up with the sound of insects and scattering of birds before it falls silent once more. The secrets of this ancient clearing remain shrouded—tales of forbidden knowledge, lost loves, and desperate bargains. The night-gaunt pulls his cocks and extra limbs out of me, splashing blood onto the ground along with the excess of his release, indifferent to my suffering.

Is it strange for envy to course through me at the thought of him waiting for his next victim? The bitter taste of jealousy morphs into rage when his non-face shimmers into that of my sister's husband, his expression cruel and contorted.

"You'll never be her. Did you really think I wouldn't be able to tell? You wretched woman. No one wants you. *I* especially will never want you."

With a spiteful cry and last burst of energy, I wildly claw at the night-gaunt's face like a possessed woman, his chilling laughter reverberating with multi-voices in amusement. Each scratch I land only results in his flesh knitting together until he once again dips his head and continues to feast leisurely. My heartbeat begins to slow, my breathing decreasing to deleterious levels.

Alone in my torment, I merge with the darkness, my spirit becoming one with the night-gaunt. My sacrifice, a warning to those who dare seek what lies beyond the veil. For in the heart of the forest, where shadows dance and sanity is unraveled, the price is always too high.

And so, the song of tormented screams plays on, my voice now among them—an eternal lament, haunting and beautiful, resounding through the ages.

THE RITUAL OF THE CALLING

S.L. SINCLAIR

This story is the direct sequel to "Innsmouth Aquarium" by Lily Luchesi, featured in Fractured Mind Publishing's *More Lore From the Mythos Volume 2.*

Felicity Marsh woke on her first day of grad school with that deep, inhuman, unearthly voice ringing in her head.

When she was little, she had dreams of fish people, of an interdimensional demon with tentacles and a wheezing voice. Her therapist insisted it was an overactive imagination combined with the stress of accidentally being locked up overnight in the aquarium when she was little, where a giant octopus was kept for study.

Over time, the dreams faded until she no longer saw Mr. and Mrs. Fishy, or the Old One who spoke prophecies over her. But every so often, she heard HIS voice.

Cthulhu.

She could not see him in her memories any longer,

nor did she truly remember his name. It was as if the wind whispered it to her when she woke, as deep as his voice and only understandable by those who were Called.

Whatever being Called meant.

As she left her apartment to get to Miskatonic University (Illinois Chapter), she found herself thinking about all the times growing up when she felt alone and out of place, and she'd call up the voice in her mind. Whenever her mind got the most tenuous grasp on it, comfort and power filled her veins. She was no longer a bullied girl, filled with anxiety and pain, but a divine being able to conquer anything in her path.

The feeling faded, but still stayed somewhere within her. She just wished she could bring it up at will and hold onto it for a decent amount of time. Especially dealing with her grad school Marine Biology professor.

Getting accepted into the brand new chapter of Miskatonic was a dream come true. Felicity learned it was next to impossible to get in, and it was odd they even opened a second chapter in America, with the first one being in Massachusetts. Indeed, all classes were small, with less than fifteen students each. Undergrads often didn't make it to their grad school, and only Felicity came there after graduating from another university entirely.

Not to mention how many students went missing after exploration expeditions.

But her professor seemed to particularly dislike her, and she didn't know why. Usually, there was a reason. The way she was blunt and quiet, an effect from being neurodivergent, was most common these days. The fact she was Black was the second most common, or rather, sometimes it fed into the other even more.

However, she wasn't the only Black kid in her class, nor was she the one with the most unique personality.

Professor Banks just seemed to despise her. No rhyme or reason.

She glanced over at the lake as she walked into the school. Miskatonic sat on the shores of Lake Michigan, and the lake, to her, was always a sight to behold. This day, it was overcast and humid, the air heavy. The water reflected the gray skies, and the waves beat against the shores and the rocks bordering land and water.

Heavy. Waiting. As if a storm was on the rise. Yet the news said it was supposed to be clear today, no storms in sight. The hair on her arms and the back of her neck stood on end, and she watched the waters, transfixed.

"Felicity..."

That voice.

As if the lake itself was calling to her, beckoning.

"Come home..."

She took a step forward, heading off the path that led to the school. Heading towards the voice. Towards home.

A hand on her shoulder, tapping it impatiently,

roused her from her reverie, and the spell that seemed to take hold vanished as fast as it had fallen.

"Miss Marsh, the lecture begins in ten minutes. I advise you to not be later than the professor," Professor Banks barked, stalking away, into Miskatonic.

Felicity glanced once more at the waters, but they were silent now. Still tumultuous, but no longer did something beyond the waves whisper her name.

For now.

She followed the professor and sat down right before the lecture began, this one on extinct aquatic creatures.

"Now, the Innsmouth Aquarium installation here in Chicago has maintained their stance on a thorough search for extinct fossils or even carcasses, or perhaps some distant, living relative in the deepest recesses of Lake Michigan. For eighteen years now, they have gathered specimens, done studies, and devoted their research to keeping the lake safe and healthy for the current inhabitants.

"While not saltwater, Lake Michigan has unique properties that allows certain species to survive, though not thrive, per se. There has been much debate on their Elder Project, which has them holding large, ancient sea creatures for study at the aquarium itself, which does contain salt water.

"One of the things I want you to research is the

effects of manufactured salt water versus natural salt water…"

Felicity's mind began to wander then, to her dreams of when she was locked in the aquarium eighteen years ago, when the Elder Project was new.

Was it really just an old octopus? Her brain felt as if something pushed against it, trying to break through. Pulsing; she began to get a headache.

"Return to us…"

"Come home, Felicity…"

The voices. These were two new ones, not the same unearthly thing, yet still inhuman. Still Calling her.

"Miss Marsh!" Professor Banks snapped. "See me after classes end."

Shit, caught daydreaming again, Felicity thought, pouting. Her classes didn't end until past five in the afternoon.

"Rough luck," N'yel, one of her classmates, commented as he and his sister, M'yel, exited the class with Felicity. "I wanted to go wave watching with you two later." He tucked some of his long, curly blond hair behind his ear.

"Maybe it's for the best," M'yel commented with a sigh. Felicity wondered what that meant, but didn't ask.

"We can go later, after this meeting," she suggested. "Meet me outside her office?"

The twins nodded, N'yel winking at Felicity with eyes that mimicked the lake outside: a gorgeous, deep gray-green shade. His sister's, on the other hand, looked like the lake in the summer mornings, bright blue and sparkling.

When that time came, Felicity walked to Professor Banks' office, but it was empty.

Wait.

Not empty. Behind the bookshelf, which was now moved slightly, was a door. Candlelight flickered from inside, and her endless curiosity was piqued.

Silent as the grave, she crept forward, peering behind the doorway. It was a small room, the walls painted a deep green with black markings all over. They looked like runes, but none she could recall seeing before. Yet, she could read them. They were for protection and guidance from the Old Ones. Just like before.

The surface was engraved with letters and markings she did not recognize. They looked like they came out of a movie about ancient civilizations. Yet somehow, she knew them. Somewhere deep in her mind, they were familiar.

She covered her mouth before a gasp could escape.

The Old Ones!

The creature in the aquarium, an Elder God from beyond time and space, locked up to be studied by scientists who had no idea what they were doing. Mr. and Mrs. Fishy, the last two Deep Ones remaining, thanks to the scientists trapping their kind in shark-infested, fake salt water.

"You will heed My Call..."

The Call. *His* Call.

How could she have forgotten? Mr. Penguin, her new plushie, falling into the deep tank, only to be rescued, presented back to her by a gigantic, pulsating tentacle. Mr. and Mrs. Fishy and their kindness. The only creatures to ever treat her like a human … and they were far from human.

"It's just your vivid imagination, Felicity," her therapist told her when she spoke animatedly about Cthulhu and the Deep Ones. "These pills will make it all go away."

No. They made her stop remembering, sure, but you can't chase reality away, no matter how uncomfortable it is.

Another voice finally hit her ears, a more familiar, human one. The professor. Peering further into the room, Professor Banks knelt at an altar lit by numerous black candles, which created the glow. Mostly.

There was also a greenish glow from the altar before her.

"What is this?" she gasped. "Finally, are you allowing me into your ways? To learn your secrets, Old One?"

A loud yet faint roar swept through the small room. *"NO."*

"What are you saying, O Great One? I can't understand you!" Frustration tinged her voice, even as she tried to be conciliatory.

I understood it fine, Felicity thought. *Just like I can read the runes.*

The voice boomed again, *"NOT FOR YOU!"*

It seemed Professor Banks understood it this time. Was it deliberately speaking English? Felicity couldn't tell the difference. Another flash of memory hit, something repressed thanks to years of therapy and medication.

Can you hear me?

"We all can." This answer came from Mrs. Fishy.

All?

The creature nodded, its massive head making waves in the water.

How do you do that? No one can ever hear me, it seems.

Mr. Fishy replied, "You speak the language of the Old Ones, little girl. A language few are privileged to know, yet many seek to learn."

"Who is it for, then? Who, if not me, your humble servant who has dedicated her life to you?" Professor Banks screeched, sounding angry, shrill, and desperate.

Without thinking, Felicity stepped fully into the room and said, "It's for *me*."

The candle flames jumped, increasing in size, the flames changing from orange to green, causing the room to glow as if they were in the lake itself.

Professor Banks whirled around, eyes narrowing when she saw Felicity.

"You? You think you, a mere child, deserve to know the language of the Old Gods?"

"I don't have to think it," she replied. "They chose me."

"The Young One," the voice echoed.

"Dammit, I cannot understand you!" the teacher snapped. "Speak to me!"

There was a laugh from somewhere behind Felicity, and she spun around to see N'yel and M'yel standing in the doorway to the hidden room.

Had it been that long already?

"What are you doing here?" Professor Banks scolded. "Get out right now!"

"Oh, I think we have a right to be here, with Our Lord's book, than you," N'yel commented. "Reading the works, the magick, of Cthulhu and Yog-Sothoth, which my sister and I painstakingly translated into your bland and common *English* centuries ago, once the Greeks finished giving it the title of *Necronomicon?*"

Banks laughed. The condescending sound was out of place here in this altar room. "Are you taking marine biology or creative writing?"

"What we are taking, Professor dear, is our freedom back," M'yel stated, her blue eyes going brighter in the candlelight. "Felicity, you can still understand the Old One?"

Felicity nodded. "How do you know?"

They looked at each other and smiled.

"We counted on you not recognizing us. Truthfully, it has been centuries since we appeared human — or were human," N'yel admitted. "We have watched over you from afar, as much as we could. But the closer you got to where the Calling Scrolls were held, the closer Cthulhu demanded we'd be to you. To ensure you heard the Call."

"*Cthulhu naflfhtagn,*" M'yel said, and this time Felicity could hear the difference between English and whatever language this was.

"Cthulhu no longer waits dreaming," was what she said.

"How do you speak R'lyehian?" Banks asked, her voice even higher.

M'yel smirked at her brother and he nodded.

"Because, you egotistical land-dweller, we belong to the Old Gods." N'yel began changing first, and his sister was not far behind.

Long, flowing hair changed to what looked like wet algae against pale green, scale-covered faces. They had no more ears, instead the sides of their heads, close to the jaw, sported gills. Their clothes tore as their bodies grew, also turning green. N'yel's was a bit brighter than his sister's, but both were roughly the shade of fresh-picked olives.

Only their eyes remained the same.

Felicity and Banks both gasped, but for vastly different reasons.

"Mr. and Mrs. Fishy?" Felicity blurted out. The kind creatures who helped her communicate with Cthuhlu eighteen years ago.

"What did you just call the Deep Ones?" Banks said. "Are you insane?"

Likely, Felicity thought.

"Don't behave as though you have respect for us," M'yel snapped. "You are part of the contingency who used the Old Ones' magick to imprison him here! You are the reason all Deep Ones who were transported died. How we survived, I will never understand."

"For her," N'yel whispered. "For the Young One to emerge. The same reason your Cult took our Lord: because you wished to be the one to wake him from his dreaming. But you did not. He has been awake almost since we arrived here."

Banks' eyes widened. "That is a lie!"

"He woke when the Young One appeared, lost and tearstained." N'yel advanced forward, leaving a trail of ooze behind him, and lifted Felicity's chin so she stared up into his inhuman visage. "Felicity Marsh. The One who shall save Cthulhu, create Deep Ones once more, and take revenge for indignities suffered."

"Dexter Ward once called for Death, and our dear god Yog-Sothoth answered. This time, it is the gods who call for Death," M'yel added. "And rebirth."

Banks fell to her knees, startling them all. "Please. Please tell our Old Gods I am a faithful servant! I will renounce my ways with the Elder Project and help exact revenge. I will do what a child such as this cannot!" She gestured to Felicity, and something clicked inside of her mind.

"You knew."

All three looked at her in confusion.

She stepped towards Banks, still on her knees. "You knew I was Called. That's why you hated me, tried to get me expelled, change majors… You didn't want me taking what's rightfully mine!"

Banks glared at her and went to stand, but her body only twitched. "What did you do to me?"

"Just a little old magick," N'yel said, leaning against the altar, while M'yel combed over its contents.

"The Calling Scrolls. I knew they were here!" she said, holding up what looked like vellum triumphantly. "Felicity, these are yours. Did you not see the lake today? The time is now to Awaken, Young One. But you don't have to do this. It may be … unpleasant."

"Or it may be great fun," N'yel commented. "There is a multi-step ritual, and once you do this … you will never return to the way you are now."

She glanced at them. "Will I become like you?"

They shook their heads, slime splattering around them.

"You will have some small changes, some new powers, however your form will not change fully unless you will it to. And even then, it would be more like

Cthulhu than us," N'yel replied. He reached for something on the altar and brought forth a beautiful obsidian blade, its handle encrusted with sparkling green gems.

"Tell me, Professor Banks, are you a true servant of Cthulhu?" he asked.

She nodded.

"Do you truly wish to aid in completing his Awakening Ritual?"

"Yes!" she cried. "Yes, I will do anything for our Lord!"

N'yel's no-lipped mouth curled into a smile, revealing small fangs all throughout. "Good." He handed the blade to Felicity. "Step one of the Calling Ritual. We must collect the Blood of the Believer. Or, rather, the Called must collect it."

He didn't mean…

Felicity looked at him, silent, then at the knife, and her eyes landed on Professor Banks, who looked as if she was ready to collapse. The only thing holding her up was his spell. And Felicity knew her mental question was already answered: N'yel meant for her to kill her professor.

Felicity had a hard time killing spiders and mosquitos. How could she kill a human being.

Blood pounded in her ears, and she felt breathless. Her palms began to perspire.

Was she scared … or excited?

"All those who Believe yet participate in things which harm us and our Lord must be punished. This way, at least she can be of use," M'yel explained. "All it needs to do is coat the knife, but the blood won't activate unless you take her life. Her soul's release from this plane will allow it to go into the Void, then her blood shall be useful."

Felicity hesitated, her hand hovering over the knife, before she gripped it firmly. It felt cold and slimy after being in N'yel's hand, but she didn't dare try to wipe the slime off.

"No, no, you cannot do this," Banks pleaded.

"You should be happy: you're about to finally be of service to your god," Felicity commented.

With one hand, she yanked the professor's head up by her hair, and with the other she sliced her throat from ear to ear. The blade stabbed the carotid first, and Banks let out a wheezing gag, eyes bulging. Slowly, ever so slowly, Felicity sliced, blood raining down like a waterfall over the professor's sagging skin.

Banks gasped and gurgled, then the spell on her body broke, and she fell to the floor in a growing pool of warm, fresh blood.

"Good girl," N'yel praised. "M'yel, bring the scrolls. Felicity … I need you to hold on tight to me and keep the knife aloft. We cannot have the blood wash away. Understood?"

Felicity nodded.

"Let us begin phase two," M'yel said, eyes alight with dark glee.

N'yel grasped Felicity and held her tightly to his chest. Their bodies both shielded the knife without wiping away the blood as the trio exited Miskatonic and went outside into the darkness.

Clouds blanketed the sky, darker gray than Lake Michigan, which was even more tumultuous. Waves crashed and water roared; not even a lone seagull dared to fly. The air was still heavy. Waiting.

Except now so was Felicity. Waiting to finish her Calling.

The siblings jumped into the lake, wading and swimming with their torsos above water to get to a small expanse of concrete the city built long ago to help divert water away from Lake Shore Drive.

N'yel laid Felicity down on the wet concrete, and both of them stood over her.

"Begin this chant here," M'yel said, showing Felicity the Scroll. "We will echo you, then we will begin. Once we are done ... *he* will appear."

There was no need to ask who "he" was.

Felicity took the Scroll, and M'yel gestured for the knife in a trade, which Felicity gave without question. The Scroll was also in R'lyehian, but she understood every word.

"Today, the One who is Called to the highest order has arrived.

"Today the Young One Awakens, and in doing so, Reawakens and frees our Old God, Cthulhu, from the dreaming.

"In a Ritual of Blood and Life, of Death and Rebirth, let the Young One bring forth a new age of R'lyeh on this accursed Earth.

"Open yourself to the bone, Young One, and welcome in the Old Gods' magick to revive you and make you in the image of our own Cthulhu."

N'yel and M'yel repeated the sentences after she said them, and as they spoke, the lake became more volatile, water washing over them all, soaking her clothes and plastering them to each and every curve.

"I will begin, and my sister will finish the Ritual with you," N'yel said after the chanting was done. "This will hurt."

"No physical pain can match what they made me feel my whole life," Felicity admitted. "They made me think I was mad."

"They did the same to us, when we were human and heard the Call of the Deep," M'yel admitted. "And now, you can have your revenge on behalf of us all."

N'yel got to his knees before her and his webbed-fingered hands were on her t-shirt. This was not what Felicity expected, and panic built up within her for a different reason.

"Wait! Please, I—"

"It matters not. This body, the soul it houses,

belongs to Cthulhu, and the Called cannot rebuke his desires." With that, he rendered her shirt in two, her bra as well, revealing her full, round breasts to the humid air. Water washed over them, ensuring she was soaked.

N'yel did the same to her pants and panties, not gentle whatsoever. His beautiful eyes stared with hard concentration as the pupils dilated with lust. Yet when he touched her, it was with reverence. "Amazing what beauty will walk amongst our ranks. None will be able to resist our Young God."

"We certainly can't," M'yel added. She stroked her triangular anal fin, like a female fish has, and Felicity realized she was getting herself off at the sight of her brother's depravity.

Felicity wished to protest more; this wasn't how she thought this would happen, and doubt and fear clouded her mind.

"Hold … still," came the booming, echoing voice in her head. *"You will suffer … for my sake."*

N'yel left tracks of slime all over as he caressed her, and finally he held her thighs open and positioned his long, impossibly thick anal fin at Felicity's entrance.

It won't fit, she thought, horrified. *He'll kill me.*

"That's the point," N'yel said, hearing her thoughts. "Death. Rebirth. Revenge."

The fin was coated in slime, making passage easier for him as he pushed the tip inside. At first, it wasn't so bad, and Felicity made the mistake of relaxing. With one strong, final thrust, he shoved the rest of it inside of her, and her screams echoed out over the empty lake, and the water responded to her pain, crashing harder, tearing rocks off the coast, pouring onto the paved streets.

"That's it. Do you feel that? Bleed for your master, bleed for your Lord. Suffer so that you can be reborn to lead us, Young One," N'yel said, thrusting deep, in and out, in time with the crashing waves.

Felicity was crying, no longer screaming, as slime and blood eased the pain a bit. She should fight, she knew this, but she couldn't.

This was her destiny. She was Called. And after she gained her powers, she would get revenge on many — N'yel included.

Pressure built within her, her nipples tightened, and shame hit as her orgasm rushed through her, tearing more cries from her throat. How could there be pleasure in this? How could her body be able to respond as the fin wriggled and invaded, tearing her just a bit?

N'yel stilled, pulsing as something, what felt like more slime, released inside of her. The cold, clammy feel of it raced through her body, spreading from between her legs, inside her bleeding cunt, through her veins.

Taking over her.

He pulled out, tail glistening with slime, blood, and her release.

M'yel then got to her knees as N'yel stood up. Felicity watched, motionless as the coldness continued to take her over, as M'yel began to lick her brother's fin clean, moaning at the taste.

She then turned to Felicity, admiring her. "Your pain will make your rebirth even stronger, Young One," she promised. The blood-soaked knife, held in one slimy hand, waved before Felicity's eyes.

The next thing she knew, the blade was unceremoniously shoved inside of her, and her screams made her throat ache. M'yel used the knife like a cock, thrusting with it, slicing Felicity open from the inside while she screamed and begged for it to stop.

But it wouldn't stop.

They came too far to stop now. If they did, this all would have been for nothing.

"Blood of the Believer," M'yel said. "Take the Blood within yourself to bind your spirit, your existence, to the other Believers. Solidify yourself as a god, Felicity. Bleed for them as they shall bleed for you."

Her vision swam, and finally, blessedly, the knife stopped plundering her. N'yel and M'yel began to clean it, licking it, before offering the tip of it to her.

"Taste it. Drink it in," N'yel commanded.

Afraid they may cut her tongue if she refused, Felicity did as she was told. Immediately, her tongue and face went as cold and clammy as the rest of her.

I'm dying, she thought.

"No," N'yel answered in her mind. *"You're Awakening."*

There was a great crash, and Felicity turned her head to see the aquarium wall, the one that faced the lake, where Cthulhu had been kept prisoner, blow apart. Gray bricks fell into the ocean, dust flitting through the air as great waves began to churn, wiping away more of the building.

The ground, the lake floor itself, rumbled, and she knew it was time.

Cthulhu was free.

The water pulsed and flowed, the current heading towards them.

The gigantic, reddish purple head breached the water, soaking all three of them.

He was magnificent, terrifying, horrible. No words could come to Felicity as she beheld the Elder God with her own eyes.

As he floated from the ocean, the skies burst open, drenching everything in freezing cold rain.

He had two bulbous eyes that seemed covered with cataracts, yet Felicity felt them stare at, within, and through her. There were wings; great, batlike wings, keeping him midair. His body rippled, muscle and flesh, sturdy enough to withstand a missile it seemed. Thirteen long tentacles floated, eager to grasp something. The suckers pulsated all on their own. There were barely healed wounds on his body, and Felicity felt a pang of pity.

"I ... am ... free!" Cthulhu declared. "Let all who ... opposed me. Who ... harmed my Deep Ones... Let them tremble in fear as ... the new god awakens to take her place at my side."

His voice still wheezed, but he was stronger now. Much stronger. The sacrifices — Felicity's body, Banks' soul and blood — were working.

"The final ... stage is about to begin," he declared. "Young One, you will ... make all of R'lyeh proud."

A tentacle reached out and wrapped itself around Felicity's waist, hauling her up into the air before the Old God.

Rain pelted her, making her already cold body even colder.

She had no idea what was about to happen, yet she held no fear. No, whatever happened now, she knew it would kill her.

But it would also bring her back to life in more ways than one.

A second tentacle, then a third, came and wrapped themselves around each breast, squeezing the soft flesh. They crossed each nipple, and a suction cup began to pulsate on them both.

Her bleeding cunt was filled once again; this tentacle bigger than N'yel's fin. It had a mind of its own, it seemed, as it pushed into places it should not have been able to reach, making her body bulge. It stroked her walls, and a sucker pressed against her g-spot.

A fifth tentacle slid behind the other, pressing into her rear hole.

"No!" she cried. "It can't—"

Her screams cut off her words as the tentacle breached that hole, tearing into her, undulating in her guts. Filling her so that she was more Cthulhu than she was herself.

A sixth and final tentacle invaded her mouth, her throat, cutting off air flow as she tried to remember to breathe through her mouth. If it went any deeper, that tentacle and the one in her guts may have met in the middle.

Cthulhu filled her, overtook her, using her body as nothing but a puppet, a toy. She didn't feel like a god; she felt like a used napkin someone threw in the trash. Her body was torn apart from the inside, and yet a deep, dark part of her mind loved this and wanted more. Wanted Cthulhu to completely rend her asunder and rebuild her in his image. To destroy the last vestiges of her humanity, to replace her pain with pleasure.

To become One with the Elder God.

The eldritch horror began to tremble and shake, before something shot out of the suckers on its tentacles into all three of her orifices. The ones on her skin, the substance began to burn away at her, leaving her flesh bare and bloody, soaked with his release.

She could not scream. Or escape.

All she could do was die.

Blackness. Floating. Space. It was cold, but she couldn't feel it. It was more like an instinctive knowledge. There were dark galaxies here, one of which's pattern of stars and nebulas looked like Cthulhu's flesh.

She felt nothing.

Am I dead?

Before her came a whorl of light, taking shape to form a person. Taking the shape of ... her.

But this was not Felicity Marsh. No, Felicity Marsh was dead. This was ... this was the spirit of the Young One.

"Are you ready?" the spirit of light asked.

"For what? I'm dead," Felicity replied, as simple as if she were to say, "I'm hungry."

"Your human self died," the light replied. "I survived. Are you prepared to embrace me and become the dark god they always feared?"

Felicity opened her mouth to respond, when there was a vicious tug on her consciousness, and back to her broken body she went, still held up high in Cthulhu's tentacle.

Her flesh and skin began to knit back together, and where it knitted, new dark purple hues emerged, matching with the Elder God. It was stark against her dark skin, blending like CGI, enhancing her beauty, even as her face and her very eyes changed color as they regenerated.

Cthulhu killed her.

And his powers remade her.

No. Not quite.

She remade herself. She chose to return. She was born for this.

There was a terrible pain in her back and she yelled to the night sky as wings sprouted, and from within, along her sides, tentacles grew. Just six, three on each side, but every bit as strong and deadly as Cthulhu's.

"Our ... Young One," Cthulhu said proudly. *"It has been so many millennia ... yet you are here."*

"I am here." Felicity could speak no longer. Instead, her voice echoed like his did. It was everywhere, everything. It was sound and meaning and silence. She turned to stare at N'yel and M'yel, her Mr. and Mrs. Fishy.

"And now, it is time for revenge."

FIN. (pun intended)

INTO THE DEEP

STEPHANIE ELLIS

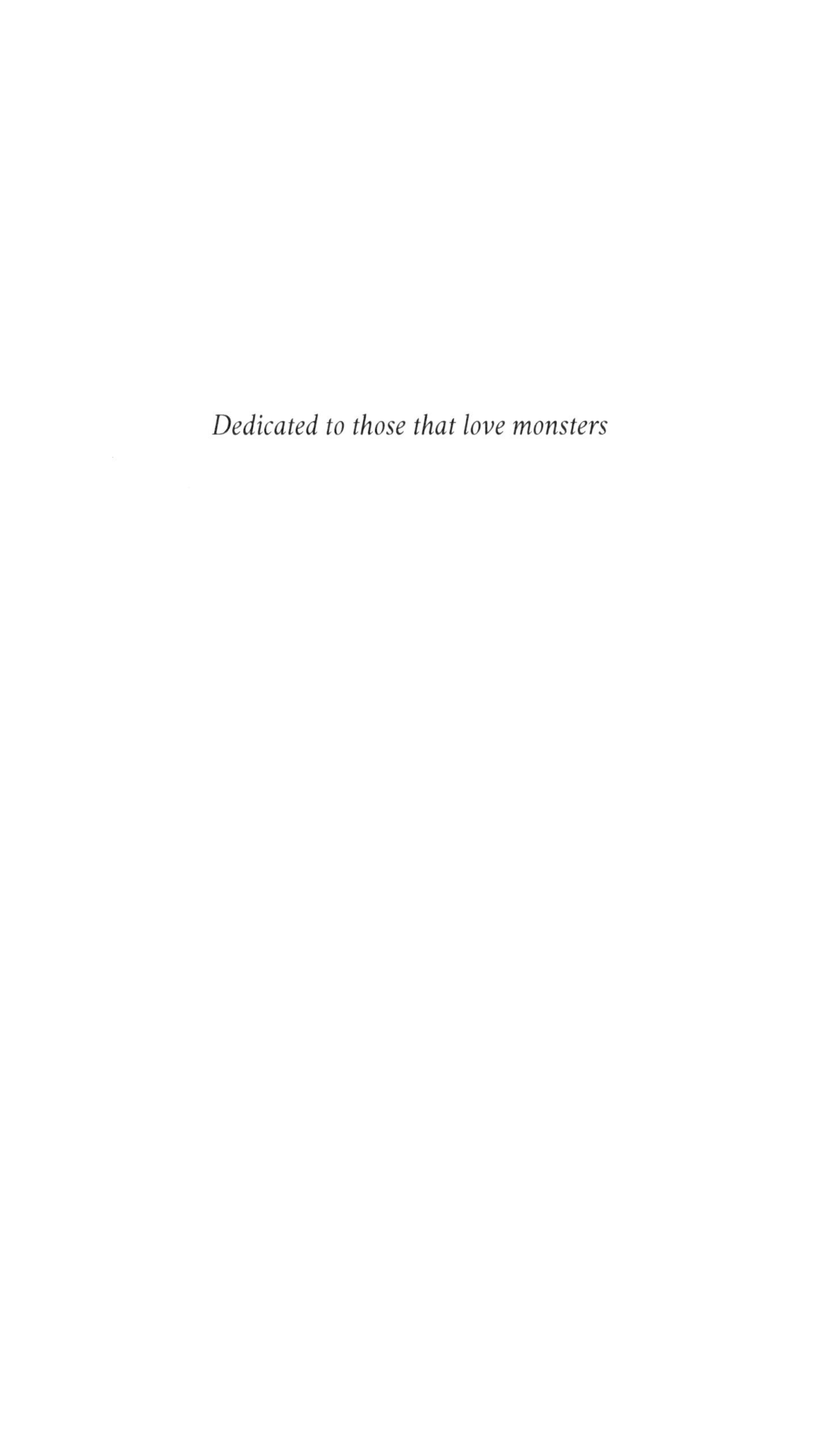

Dedicated to those that love monsters

TRIGGER WARNING

Please be mindful of the following potential triggers that are included in this story:

Non-Con

1
NIALL

I put my car in park and sigh. I can hear them in my head. The croaks, the groans, the calls to come home. It's almost time for me. My time is almost done but I don't want to go.

However, I have no choice. It's never been my choice; it's going to happen. I knew all about this, and yet I left Innswick to see if I could outrun it. No dice.

I wanted a normal life, but I'm not normal. For the last ten years, I've lived life to the fullest, I think. I moved out at eighteen, went to college—much to the protest of my dad— had fun there, played video games and sports. Then I met someone. I fell in love with her.

We got married. She has no idea who I am, or what is happening to me. Though she knows something is wrong, as I've been distant to her. Since the change is already happening, I can't let her see me, well, see what's happening underneath my clothes.

Without her knowledge, I just quit my job. She's inside making my favorite seafood dish and I'm sitting in my car like a coward. I don't want to hurt her, but I'm going to have to.

Turning the car off, I head inside with a heavy heart and voices in my head. I guess they're not really voices, but sounds, ones I understand.

The smell of crab legs and butter hits my nose upon entering and I almost smile. My perfect wife rounds the corner.

"Oh yay, you're home."

I do smile at her and set my wallet and keys on the side table, knowing what I must do, but letting us have this one night together before I end up blowing it up to kingdom come.

"Is dinner ready?" I ask and she nods, jerking her head toward the table. She's already set it, even putting my favorite beer in front of my plate. She always takes good care of me.

"How was work today?" she asks as she piles crab legs onto my plate before handing it to me. She goes back for cheddar biscuits, though they aren't my cup of tea.

"It was okay." I shrug.

She stares at me for a moment before asking. "Is everything okay?"

I push my plate back and come up with an excuse. "I have to go visit home for a bit, my dad is sick."

She frowns. "Oh, no. I'm so sorry to hear that. When are you going? Do you want me to come with you? I can take off work."

I shake my head. "I'm leaving tomorrow morning. I know this is last minute."

She pats my arm, and I want to curl up and die right there; she's just so kind.

"I understand. I can come with you."

Again, I shake my head. "No, you stay here. I'll only be a week or so." Lie.

She gives me a sweet smile. "You take care of your dad. If you need me, though, I'll come."

I don't deserve her. I never did.

"Thanks. How was your day?"

"It was good. Just long." She works at a high-end retail store. She loves it and just got promoted. We celebrated with a night out when she got the call she got the promotion. I'm really proud of her.

"We can eat and then relax on the couch," I suggest and her eyes light up. The rest of dinner is small talk and gossip about the neighbors. When we're finished, I send her to the living room so I can clean up.

LEXI

Niall has been acting weird for a few days. I'm sad to hear about his father, though. Maybe that's what has been wrong. I've spoken to my father-in-law on the phone, but we've never met. Neither my husband nor his father talk about his mother. I brought it up once, and he told me not to ask again. I never did.

I just want us to be how we were before last week, cute and cuddly. I'm going to miss him while he's gone. It kind of hurts that he doesn't want me to go with him.

With that thought, an idea forms in my head, I'll show up and surprise him. I haven't had a vacation in a year, so I have the time off. And through this difficult time, he's going to need me. And if I just show up, he can't turn me away.

I feel the couch sink and I turn and smile at my perfect husband. "What do you want to watch?"

He tucks a piece of hair behind my ear. "Something sappy."

See? Perfect man.

I choose some sappy romance and let it play while I lay down, my head in his lap. I love times like this with him, just the two of us.

He plays with my hair; I love when he does that. Soon, I fall asleep in the arms of the man I love.

3

NIALL

I watch her sleep. It's early morning and I need to be on my way. She looks so beautiful and peaceful. She doesn't need me, doesn't need this. I should have listened to Dad and never left. This is misery and torture.

Leaning down, I kiss her cheek and leave the house, wiping the tears as I get in my car. The sounds in my head are louder and it's time, I can't wait.

The drive isn't long, in fact it's a mere two-hour drive. Lexi doesn't know that I visited my dad when I told her I was out running errands. Again, lies upon lies.

I guess love makes us do stupid things.

By sunlight, I'm pulling into Dad's driveway and, by a miracle, the sounds have lessened. Thank Dagon; they gave me a headache.

Dad opens the door and gestures for me to come in. I grab my bag and enter my childhood home. Being back here brings back memories, some good, some bad.

I never knew my lineage until I was seventeen. I was raised like all the other kids in the area. But right before my eighteenth birthday, Dad sat down and told me who my mother was, and what was going to happen to me.

The whole town knew, though no one treated me differently. In fact, some people were nicer. Dad and I went to church, and I was always in what I guess could be called Sunday school. Sundays are hazy for me as I really didn't pay attention. But Dad told me that this church was special.

I'm special to a degree and that's why the townsfolk are nice to me. The sounds in my head and myself are crucial to the town surviving.

To some that might sound like I'm a hero, but in reality, I'm not.

"You hungry? I'm making breakfast," Dad says, pulling me back to the present.

I nod. "I could eat."

My breakfast is different from his, scrambled eggs with crickets. Gross right? But when I noticed the change, I also found myself wanting things that weren't normal for humans. Dad knows this because he's been the only one I can be open and honest with. Okay, I know some humans like chocolate-covered crickets and grasshoppers, but for me, it's what sustains me.

"How's Lexi?" Dad asks, putting my eggs and crickets in front of me along with a large glass of water. Lately I found I need lots of water, more than just eight cups a day. But water's good for you, right?

I hang my head a little bit. "I didn't tell her. I chickened out. She'll report me missing and hopefully they'll declare me dead so she can collect insurance."

He shakes his head. "I'm not going to say it again."

He wants to say, 'I told you so.' But he would sound like a broken record.

"I know."

He sits down to eat and takes a long look at me. "Are you scared?"

"Terrified. I have so many questions and will I be able to come visit?"

He sighs. "I don't have the answers."

I know he doesn't, and it's not like he can ask my mom. Until I was born, he was under some kind of spell that these things have on the townsfolk. Back then he thought it was an honor to be picked to mate with them.

I'm not sure what happened, but now he knows not to say anything against the sea creatures. That's what I will become, a sea creature.

A fish man, a man fish. A Deep One.

The lore has been that the Deep Ones help run down towns along the coast. They bring in fish so the markets can sell them. They bring treasure to trade or sell. Small towns prosper under their watchful eyes.

And if someone speaks ill about them, that person becomes a sacrifice. The town spins it as they sacrifice to help the town. That person is never spoken about again.

Men in the city and some women volunteer to mate, to bring life because if the Deep Ones are happy, the town is happy.

Hybrids, like me, don't see the change until late twenties, early thirties. It's gradual and everyone goes through it differently.

For me? I'm starting to change color, which is why I didn't want Lexi to see me without clothes on, which sucks because sex with her is amazing.

I'm about to ask him a question when there is a knock on the door.

I hold my hand up. "I'll get it."

I head to the front door and nearly fall over when I see who is standing on my doorstep.

"Thought I would come help," Lexi says and I almost collapse.

4

LEXI

Niall doesn't look well; he looks scared to see me. Looking over his shoulder, his dad even looks horrified, worried even.

John, Niall's dad, clears his throat. "Bring her inside so the neighbors don't see."

Huh? What does that mean? But before I can ask, Niall pulls me inside and slams the door, asking, "Why are you here?"

He sounds livid and we've never fought.

I try to step closer, but he steps back. "I came to surprise you. Surprise."

My voice wavers on the last word and maybe I shouldn't have come. But I love Niall; we told ourselves through sickness and health.

John glances over at me. "I'll make another plate."

I'm guessing I interrupted breakfast. My stomach growls and Niall just walks away.

Before I follow, I turn around the room, taking in the photos along the wall. I take in the photos of him growing up, all the way through to the one of us from our wedding. That was the happiest day of my life, even if his dad couldn't be there. This man is my whole life and from the look on his face, he's keeping something from me.

Sighing, I turn on my heel and walk in the direction he disappeared. John's kitchen is small but bright. Lots of open windows facing the ocean, if I had a place like this I would sit here forever with a cup of tea.

Both men sit at the table, and I join them, not sure what to say now.

"Niall, I'm sorry for springing this on you," I tell him and he shrugs.

John rubs his temples. "Might as well tell her what is going on."

Niall's head whips up. "We will sound crazy. She's not staying."

The she he is talking about and I'm right across the table from him. "Do you not want me to be here?"

He drops his head. "It's not that. You can't be here."

"Can't? That is a little weird. I took vacation days, so I think I can."

He shakes his head. "A couple of days, but don't engage with locals."

I guess I'll take that. "Will you show me around?"

He grunts and keeps eating. I've angered him enough for the day, and when I see bugs in his food, I want to say something, but don't. Maybe tonight I'll ask him why he was eating bugs, but for now I'm going to take my win.

5

NIALL

I should have told her to go the minute I opened the door, but I love my wife. I guess I will get to spend a few more days with her until everything happens.

A few days and she will be gone. Hopefully no one notices her here. She'll ask questions, they'll ask questions, it would be a shit show.

No speaks ill of the sea creatures that helped our starving town turn around and I'm sure Lexi would find it weird. It is weird. It's one of the reasons I left. I wanted to live a normal life, but I'm not normal. Never will be.

Lexi finishes her breakfast, and I take our plates to the sink, nodding at Dad when I lead her to my room. She takes in everything. She stares at the pictures on my wall, her hand brushes the worn wallpaper. Dad washed my blankets and sheet, the blanket I had from

83

when I was in middle school. I won awards at school for various competitions; they sit on a bookshelf. She looks at every single one.

She pulls one of my favorite books off the shelf, turning it over in her hand. "This is your room?"

It's an odd question because she can clearly see that it is, but I'm guessing she's caught off guard because of earlier. "It is. It's small, but I like it."

She places the book back on the shelf. "I like it." She smiles at me, the smile I fell in love with, and I pull her in for a kiss.

She wraps her arms around me and I bring her to bed; scales be damned, I need her.

She falls on to the bed and instantly starts stripping. Yeah, it's been awhile. Once she's naked, splayed out on the bed, I straddle her, leaning in for another kiss. I trail my hand down her leg, pulling it up while I lean back a little. As I kiss her, I push a finger in, finding her dripping wet.

I push my finger in and out, watching her face as she withers underneath me. "You're so beautiful."

Her response is to moan, and I know I can't wait, I need to be inside her. I back down and flick my tongue across her clit and she nearly jumps off the bed. While I keep bringing her pleasure, I drop my pants, but not my shirt. I guess I'm not ready.

I climb back up and kiss her while I slide my cock in, groaning, missing this.

"Take your shirt off," she whispers and I freeze. I go to get up, but she stops me. "Sorry. I won't ask again. I miss you, I miss the feeling of you."

I keep going, thrusting, as she cries out. I don't even care Dad can hear us, I've needed this for a long time.

Reaching down, I pinch her clit, and she comes, strangling my cock with her tight pussy, causing me to come. Less than ten minutes; that's a first for me. Usually I can go for hours, but it's been a long time since we've been together.

Breathing hard, I roll off to the side and hold her close. "There are things you don't know about me and you'll be hurt when I tell you. I'm not ready to tell you just yet, but know that I kept these secrets from you to protect you."

She flips over to face me. "We don't keep secrets."

I nod. "I know. It will all make sense. I'll tell you before you leave, but let's just have a couple of relaxing days together before the blowout."

She agrees. "Okay. Can we go to the beach?"

The beach might be okay, unless one of the neighbors decides to walk by, but I can't keep saying no to her, it will only cause more arguments. I want her to leave happy, with the knowledge that I love her.

"Okay, we can go."

She grins at me and cuddles closer as she falls asleep. A nap right now might be good.

6

LEXI

It's been so long since we've had sex, I forgot how good it was with Niall. It's not the sole reason I married him, but he knows how to make me feel pleasure, always making sure I'm taken care of.

I fell asleep happy that he was going to take me down to the beach, his weird behavior from before a thing of the past. He did say he had secrets and I should be angry with him, but he said he would come clean to me in due time.

I'll give him his time and for now I'll enjoy being around him.

But what if that secret is that he's dying? What if he cheated on me? Is his dad really sick? I know I said I wanted to give him time, but these are valid questions.

Okay, I know I'm spiraling. I said I would give him time and I will.

I roll out of his bed, which is really comfy, and pull my swimsuit out of my bag. He must have gone out to get it for me, he's a doll that man. Pulling it on, I step into my shorts and pull a shirt over my head. I don't think I'll need a jacket, it's still warm with a slight breeze. I walk back down the hallway and find Niall making sandwiches.

He sets one aside as he glances over his shoulder at me. "Hungry?"

I snort. "Someone really worked me up and over, so yeah."

He laughs. "Was it as good for you as it was for me?"

I just giggle as he points to the table. "Where's your dad?"

He tenses a little bit. "He went to get groceries."

"I could have gone and got them. I am the guest after all."

He shakes his head. "He wanted to get out of the house." He sets a plate with a sandwich and chips in front of me. He brings his over as well and I see crickets in it.

I point at his sandwich. "What's with the bugs?"

He glances at his sandwich and then back at me. "Protein."

I stare at him for a minute. "Gross."

He looks down and eats. Did I hit a nerve? Did I say something wrong? My answer seems to upset him.

Placing my hand on his arm, I say, "I'm not sure what's going on, but you eat what you want."

He pats my hand and goes back to eating. When we're finished, he takes our plates to the sink and jerks his head toward the back door.

He slides it open and I can see that the deck wraps around to the side of the house and there are stairs that go all the way down to the beach. The wood is worn, but they still look sturdy. The water is blue, and small waves hit the shore. Shells are all about, sun high in the sky. Looking over at my husband, I see he's wearing one of his favorite shirts. It's blue and worn. It was one of the first shirts I bought for him right after we met. He has on black swim shorts, with flip flops. He spreads out a blanket and then pats it as he sits down.

"This town isn't normal," he says.

I guess he's going to start telling me why he's been acting so off. I say nothing and let him continue, I'll save my questions for the end.

"My birth wasn't normal. My mom isn't around because she doesn't live here. Or anywhere. I'm not really sure. I knew growing up I was different, even though I look like everyone else. Let's just say I'm going through some changes and I won't look like this for long."

Umm what?

"I won't go into all the details today, but just know I'm not normal." He ends his ramble.

I chuckle a little. "Who is normal?" Everyone has their quirks.

He waves it off. "You'll soon see that I'm not your normal."

Whatever that means. I want to ask a lot more questions but a raspy voice interrupts. Looking up, an older man is walking up the beach toward us. He recognizes my husband.

And the look on my husband's face is pure terror. What the what?

7

NIALL

I hear my name being called and when I look up I see Mr. Jennings, the mayor, walking toward us. My face must show my horror because Lexi tenses up but does try to smile.

"Niall, nice to see you. You must be here for the ceremony," he says and all I can do is nod. I'm praying my dear wife says nothing so as to not draw attention to herself.

But nope, she dives right in.

"Ceremony?" she asks, giving me a curious look. Mr. Jenning now sees I'm not alone. The town is always tight-lipped about all things Innswick, only speaking about details in private, under the watchful eye of Dagon.

Turning toward her, I reply, "It's a festival we have every year."

Mr. Jennings gives her a creepy smile. "And who are you?"

Lexi smiles and holds out her hand. "I'm Lexi, Niall's wife."

I can feel the mayor's eyes on me as he talks to her. "Is this your first time visiting?"

She nods. "I love it here. It's so peaceful."

I cringe inwardly as Mr. Jennings takes a seat. "We take pride in our little oasis. How long do you plan to stay?"

She tips her head. "I'm not sure, probably just a few days. His dad isn't feeling well, so I'm here to help out."

He turns to me with a knowing look. "Your dad is sick, is he? Such a shame. We miss him at church."

Lexi pipes up. "We should go with him before I leave. Sometimes prayer helps."

Fuck my life.

Standing up quickly, I pull Lexi up. "It was nice to see you, Mayor."

I drag her behind me as she tries to pull her hand away. "That was rude. He seemed nice."

Yeah, he's not. But I can't explain that to her right now, I need her inside. It won't matter, even if she's behind closed doors, everyone in town will know there's an outsider here.

Ignoring her, I pull her inside and shut the door, locking it, before turning to her.

She shrinks back from me and at first I think it's

because she knows I'm angry. At what? I have no idea. I guess myself.

But it's when she points at my neck. "What is going on?"

I glance in the window and see that my neck now has gills, the change is happening faster than I thought. I guess being back here is what is bringing it on.

Her face is pale. "You're a monster." It comes out as a whisper, almost like she thinks she's in a nightmare that she'll wake up from.

"I can explain." My voice croaks with sadness and the change in me.

A voice behind me chimes in. "Let me, son."

Dad to the rescue.

8

LEXI

Niall has gills. Like, fish gills. What is happening? I have to be dreaming. And the man on the beach mentioned a ceremony. What is going on?

I pinch myself, hoping that this is a nightmare, but nope, I'm awake and looking at my handsome husband with gills on his neck.

John motions for me to sit at the table while he makes some tea. Niall doesn't move from where he stands, still staring in the window.

Handing me a cup of tea, John sits down with a long sigh. "I promise you what I'm about to say is all true but will sound crazy."

I nod, silently sipping my tea and waiting for him to continue. I can give him his chance to speak before I start asking questions. I'm not even sure how to feel right now.

John taps the table, then he starts, "Innswick is not your normal town. Decades ago, the townsfolk were barely surviving. The town was basically falling apart. And then one day this entity, not sure what else to call him, appeared. Dagon. He and his fish men could bring the town back from the brink. When everything started turning around, Dagon was worshipped, cheered."

"Who is Dagon?" I interrupt him.

He continues, "Dagon is something otherworldly. In layman's terms, a mermaid. He's half-human, half-fish. He's huge and terrifying. So, not a nice mermaid."

I place my hand on the table. "You're telling me you worship a fish?"

I start to laugh but notice that they're faces are serious.

"Don't speak ill of Dagon," John warns me, then goes on like I said nothing. "The change you see in Niall is shocking, I understand. With the wealth that started to change the town, sacrifices and deals were made. We all thought it was an honor to be picked . Some of us were picked to mate; every year men are chosen. Once Niall was born, I raised him like any child, all the while knowing the change was coming. I was shunned for letting him leave, but I wanted him to experience life before everything happened."

"I'm sorry, you mated with who?"

He takes a sip of his tea. "A Deep One."

I start to laugh again. "A Deep One?"

He nods. "They're Dagon's subjects. Mermen, or frog men. They live in the sea, bringing treasure found for the city to sell. They bring in an abundance of fish to eat and sell. They saved our town. My mating with one was an honor because I got Niall. He's not normal and he will become one of them."

I sit back in my seat and stare at John.

"This is crazy, that has to be makeup; you just want to scare me." I point at Niall.

Niall shakes his head. "It's not makeup." He pulls up his shirt and I can see his skin is grey.

Standing up abruptly, I say, "This is all crazy, you're all crazy. Worshipping a fish and mating with them to create monster babies, crazy. You lied to me. I shouldn't have come here."

Grabbing my keys, I hurry out the door as John calls my name. Shock has worn off and now I'm terrified. I'm around crazy people.

Shooting out the door, I get to my car, only to find Mr. Jennings and some other strangers. "Sorry we can't let you leave."

What the hell?

9
NIALL

We are crazy. I should have told her to go home right after she showed up on Dad's doorstep. It was selfish of me to let her stay, to have a few more days with her.

But I let her stay, and now she won't be able to leave.

Mr. Jennings looks up at Dad. "John, escort her back inside, she can't leave."

I look down at the ground, not wanting to look at Lexi. I don't want to see the anger, hurt, terror on her face. Maybe at dinner we can talk, but I doubt she will listen.

The reason she can't leave is that the secret of this place can't get out, it would cause havoc in the world. Or they would lock everyone here in mental hospitals.

I have to face reality: she's the sacrifice.

Dad pats my shoulder as he escorts Lexi back to my room and then locks the door. She'll try the window but they're locked from the outside, so no dice there. I hate that it's come to this.

Once she's locked away, Dad joins me in the living room, sighing as he takes a seat in his favorite recliner. His eyes widen when he looks at me. "It's happening faster."

I nod, croaking. "I can feel the call."

The call to find my kind, the ones I'm supposed to be with.

Picking up my phone I can see my eyes are starting to shrink in, the color of my skin is a greyish color. I know the folds on my skin that look like gills as Lexi put it are just that, they are gills or will be.

Anytime someone goes through the change, they lock themselves away. Why? I have no idea, it's not like the town would say anything, they know it's the change and the sacrifice our fathers have made. I've come to terms with it and should have left my wife earlier in life. Really I should never have left, but I did and now we're all paying the consequences.

Dad turns on the TV for noise and leaves me to my thoughts. Not that I have many, only one and she's in the other room, angry and sad.

There's not much room in my head for anything else with the calls of the Deep Ones calling me. I'm sure that in a couple days the change will be in full effect. I shake my head, wondering how I'm going to fix this for Lexi.

LEXI

They locked me in here. The window is sealed shut. Tears roll down my face as I realize I'm not leaving anytime soon. I should have never come here, but I did it for love.

The man I love is not who he says he is. He's a monster.

Up until today, I didn't know such things existed. I mean I read about monsters in books and watch monster horror movies, but that's all make believe. Right?

But my husband is changing right in front of my eyes. The people here are weird, and who is Dagon?

I guess John did try to explain it to me, but I didn't listen. They're crazy. But here I am locked in a room, wondering what is going to happen to me.

I'm mid-pace when the door opens and my

husband, if I can still call him that, walks in. He looks worse than before. His eyes are bulging and his ears are smaller. His skin is grey.

His voice comes out as a croak. "Dinner is ready."

I want to run, but I'm sure I won't get far. I am hungry. I follow behind him at a distance, not sure how to react to what's going on.

Maybe I'll wake up tomorrow and this will all be a nightmare.

John sets the table as I enter and he gives me a sad smile as I take a seat.

He sets a stew on the table, and next to Niall's plate he sets a bowl of worms.

Niall explains. "I can't really eat human food, so for a year I've been mixing bugs and worms into my food."

I almost puke at his explanation but knowing I need to eat, I keep my mouth shut.

I ladle some stew into my bowl and ignore the grossness of Niall putting worms in his. I keep my head down and eat, not wanting to talk to anyone.

After about ten minutes, John breaks the silence. "You can't ever leave."

I drop my spoon. "Never? What about my life back home? My family? What do I tell them?"

He cringes when I say that and I can see there's something he's not telling me.

"Just tell them you moved," Niall says, and I turn to him with a glare.

"Tell them I moved? What about visiting them?"

John places a hand on my shoulder as he clears the table. "We can figure something out after Niall's change."

Glancing over at Niall, I ask, "When is this change over?" I know it sounds bitchy but I can't help it. I'm being held against my will.

John glances at Niall. "Tomorrow night at the ceremony."

Tomorrow seals my fate. I don't think John will be able to help me out. I know I will never leave here. When Niall tried to get me to leave when I first arrived, I should have rushed back to my car and hightailed it out of here. I'm a prisoner and probably going to be slaughtered for a cult.

Niall tries to grab my hand but I pull away. He looks hurt, but he has no idea how I'm feeling.

"I'm sorry," he croaks out, his voice sounding worse.

"You knew this was going to happen. You were just going to leave and what? Disappear? What about me?"

He looks away and I know he doesn't have an answer to that. I thank John for the meal and go back to my prison, hoping that after tomorrow I can leave.

11

NIALL

I hate all of this and there's nothing I can do. Dad would have left a long time ago if he could have. He hates this for me. I hate this for him. He raised me, knowing one day I would have to leave—forever.

Dad cleans up the dishes and tells me to go to bed. As I walk by my room, I pause, hand on the door. I wish she would let me talk to her, but right now nothing I can say will make this better. I can hear her crying behind the door and it breaks my heart.

I step away right as extreme pain hits me in my chest. It's time.

I fall to the floor as Dad rushes around the corner. My body is changing and panic sets in. There's no coming back. I can see the sadness in Dad's eyes as he helps me to the back door, knowing that the sea is calling. Maybe with my changing, they'll let Lexi go.

I hear more footsteps and Lexi steps into view. "What is happening to him?"

She's angry, yet she's still worrying about me.

I try to talk but it comes out as a croak, no words. I can't tell them how I feel or anything.

"The change," Dad tells her as I writhe on the floor.

Then all the pain stops and I turn to flee, the water calling me.

12
LEXI

I heard the commotion and rushed out of my room, only to watch the man I love turn into a monster.

I might be angry, but my heart hurts as I lose the love of my life. His dad only watched, helpless.

He writhed on the floor and then he stopped, standing up, a green fish man, whatever he is. He looked at both of us and busted through the door. I can't describe what I saw, and I actually still think I'm going crazy.

John stands in front of the busted glass, watching his son sink into the black depths of the sea, anguish and sadness etched all over his face.

Not knowing what to do and still in shock about all of this, I go in search of a broom. Does this mean I can leave?

I don't want to ask, not now when John is mourning.

I start sweeping up, needing to do something. John clears his throat. "I can do that." He takes the broom from me and goes about cleaning up. Needing something to do, I make tea. The silence fills the room, the only sound is the water boiling on the stove and the swish of the broom.

Once the water is boiling, I pour two cups of tea and wait at the table. John dumps the glass into the trash and joins me, sighing as he sinks into his seat.

"What happens now?" I ask sadly. I need guidance, not knowing how to operate without Niall.

John takes a sip from his cup. "They're still not going to let you leave. The ceremony will go on. What they do to you, I don't know. I've never been to one of the ceremonies, except the one where Niall was conceived."

That's not what I want to hear, but at least he's honest. I watch his face as a tear falls and, knowing he needs comfort right now, I reach for his hand. "He was a good man."

John nods. "I wish I could have given him a different life. I wish this wasn't his destiny."

Me too, man, me too.

He takes my empty cup and washes it out. "Probably should get some sleep."

Yeah, I don't think I'll get any sleep tonight.

13

LEXI

There's commotion outside the house and I roll out of bed to look at what is going on.

Pulling the curtain back, I can see people milling about what was once an empty street. They're walking toward the beach with lawn chairs and coolers. I would think it was another day at the beach, but I doubt that's what this is.

No, this is for the ceremony. My ceremony or death.

A knock on the door has me turning from the window. "Come in." It's not my house, but it's a normal thing to say, right?

John enters with a grim face. "Time to get ready." He doesn't finish the sentence. And that's what this feels like—a sentence. A death sentence for me because I think what they are doing is crazy. I mean I get it, kind of. If I were to leave here and speak about all of this, people would label me as crazy. This is what I get for loving my husband.

I give him a slight nod. "I'll get dressed." He closes the door and I pull on a pair of leggings and a tee shirt. Why dress up for my death? I yank on my cardigan and slip into my sandals. Let's get this over with.

I exit my room, my prison, Niall's old room, to see Mr. Jennings and some other men waiting for me. The old man smiles at me, but I don't return it. What is there to smile about?

"Follow me," he says and I do with one last glance at John who looks heartbroken and sad for me. I hope he will find peace soon.

The men surround me as I follow Mr. Jennings down to the beach, probably thinking I'm going to try and run. Where would I go? And how would I get there? They took my keys.

People sit around the beach, waiting for me and the show. One woman does give me a sympathetic look, but when I try to speak to her, she turns away from me. No help there.

Mr. Jennings stops and looks at the crowd. "We have our sacrifice for the year. Dagon will be pleased."

The crowd murmurs, "Dagon will be pleased."

"You are all crazy," I hiss to the man and he glares at me.

"Just because you don't believe what we believe

doesn't mean you have to degrade it. We don't dismiss your beliefs."

He doesn't even know what I believe.

I turn to the crowd, hoping for someone to help me. "You can make your own way. Go out into the world, see that you don't need to kill people or worship some fish."

Mr. Jennings laughs, but it's not a funny laugh. "Dagon has brought us riches beyond our belief. What has your God brought you?"

Without a beat, I say, "Love and hope. Struggles and victories, and I wouldn't change that for the world. What you have is brainwashed people."

He just shakes his head as I hear the waves pick up and some of the men whisper. "He's here."

I turn and, in true horror, something of nightmares emerges from the water. He looks like an eel with human arms, sharp teeth riding on the waves. I try to back away but someone holds my arms, stopping me in my tracks.

"Dagon, please accept our sacrifice," Mr. Jennings yells into the wind.

The monster comes closer and I turn my head, not wanting to look at it in the face.

And then the monster pulls away abruptly.

I open one eye to see monsters like Niall standing on the beach. The humans all kneel, except Mr.

Jennings and myself. I want to run but for some reason I'm rooted to where I stand.

Dagon monster looks at the fish men like they're communicating, then Dagon comes for me. Mr. Jennings is yelling praises as water surrounds me and my world goes black.

14
LEXI

The sound of ripping water stirs me as I blink, my eyes opening, then shoot up to a sitting position remembering what just happened. I'm in a cave, water dripping down the sides, light cascading through the cracks in the rock.

I look around my surroundings, grateful I'm not dead. But if I'm not dead, where am I?

This was my first time to Innswick, and I didn't get a lot of time to look around. Looking out the cave opening and seeing nothing but water doesn't help me.

The water stirs and Dagon's head pokes out, looking at me. I back up to the wall, hoping he goes away. But he doesn't.

He rises from the water and stares intensely at me. It's like he can see right through me.

I can't explain what is happening to me, but I don't

feel scared anymore. It's almost like he's telling me that I'm safe, that I was saved.

Standing, I walk to the edge and hold out my hand to him. He drops down until he's closer to me, taking a hold of my hand. Despite being whatever he is, his hand is warm.

Without warning, he gently pushes me to the cave floor and rips the rest of my ragged clothes off. I should tell him to stop, but for some reason I want this. I want him.

I close my eyes, letting me feel everything. He parts my legs and I can feel his tongue, forked tongue, set my insides on fire. Was he human in another life to know how to please me?

His tongue flicks across my clit and I let out a soft moan. While he's feasting on me, another presence takes a hold of my arms. Opening my eyes I see who I believe is Niall. His eyes are just as blue as my husband's were. Reaching out, I touch his face, and he leans in.

"Oh God," I gasp and turn my head as Dagon pushes one of his fingers into my core. I'm on fire; I need more.

Niall croaks and then changes to kneel by my head, and I instantly know what I want to do, and what he needs.

His dick is now huge and green, and for some reason

I don't care. It still feels the same, but with a saltier taste that I don't seem to mind as I suck, twirling my hand around the base. Glancing up at him, he jerks his head toward Dagon, words between them unspoken.

I turn my head slightly to see Dagon rear up and then hover closer to me, and then I see his cock. I think to myself it's not going to fit and for some reason these two beings have a chuckle, like they know what I'm thinking.

I feel full at both ends as Dagon slides his dick in and out, inch by inch until he's fully seated.

And then they pound me in both holes. And I'm here for it.

In one part of my mind, I should be running for the hills. I should be dead, or wishing I was dead.

But here I am getting pounded by two monsters and loving it. I watch Niall's webbed hand reach down and rub my clit and I come undone. I come so hard I see stars and I hear the grunts from both beings as Niall pulls out, shooting his load across the cave. Dagon roars as I come down from my high and he pulls out, slumping down into the water.

I finally get my breathing under control, then look for something to cover me. Niall beats me to it, but he brings me a blanket.

Where did he get a blanket? And what happens to me now?

Dagon huffs and nods to Niall before disappearing. Will he be back?

Niall stands and helps me up, walking toward the back of the cave. I follow, trying to figure out what's going on.

We come to a door, an actual door in the cave. Behind it is a room, I guess my room.

It has a bed, dresser, and some clothes. On the bed is a piece of paper, a note from Niall's dad.

"I know this is hard for you. Just remember you're supposed to be dead. There are other women just like you. They live somewhere in the cave, you'll have friends. And someday, you can leave. Your car is parked at an exit. The Deep Ones know you need to eat. I'll come visit someday. Whenever you do leave, avoid Innswick."

I set the letter down. I can come and go. I could just leave and never come back.

But I for some reason don't want to. And there are others? Do they do what I just did with Dagon and Niall? For some reason that makes me jealous. Niall croaks out a laugh and I glance up at him.

I see him in all his glory, and his new body. And I still love him.

He shakes his head, almost like he's telling me that Dagon wants only me and he's okay with sharing me.

His web hand reaches out, and I take it, letting him

lead me to bed. I climb up and he pulls the sheet away from me as he runs his web hand over my body.

"Love me," I whisper and his froglike tongue flicks out across my nipple.

"Fuck," I groan, needing more.

He pulls my legs apart and lowers his head, tongue rakes across my clit and I moan. He licks furiously at my core until I'm nearly sobbing with tears as I come.

He flips me over and he slams into me. I gasp. He's so big now, even though he was big as a human. He feels so good, hitting all the right spots.

"I'm coming again," I yell as I fall off the cliff, crying out his name. He doesn't let up, flipping me back over as he continues to wreak havoc on my pussy.

I stare into his eyes and give in to my new normal. I guess I'm not normal.

He comes, his croaking filling the room. As he pulls out, he pulls the blanket back over me and I curl up to sleep.

15

LEXI

I wake up with a start and snap my eyes open to see a blonde-haired girl setting clothes on the chair in the corner of the room.

She turns and smiles at me. "You're awake."

I rub my eyes for a minute, forgetting that I was almost killed by a town, had sex with two monsters, and I'm being held captive despite John's letter.

"Who are you?" I ask roughly, still processing.

She steps toward the door. "I'm Celina. I brought you clothes. Get dressed, we can have breakfast."

Breakfast? My stomach growls at that thought. Sliding out of the bed, that is very comfortable by the way, I put on the jeans and tee shirt she brought me. I find my cardigan has been washed and dried for me. I put it on for comfort. Sliding my feet into the shoes left for me, I open the door to find Celina in an embrace with one of the green fish men. When they hear the door, he hops off into the water and she blushes. "He's the one that claimed me."

I have no idea what to say to any of this. Despite the best sex of my life, I should be terrified, angry. Okay, I'm angry. But I should be scared. Why aren't I?

"Because it was meant to be," Celina states, giving me a bright smile. She leads me through a tunnel and into an open valley inside the cave. There's light from above and it's almost like a bunch of cave dwellings within the structure. But modern. Weird.

"How do you know what I'm thinking?" I ask her as we walk down some steps to a large table.

"It's what we all thought when we were sacrificed, as the townsfolk of Innswick call it. There's only about ten of us. But some of the Deep Ones didn't want Dagon to kill us. When I first arrived here, I wanted to die. But the one you found me with, he showed me that monsters can treat us better than some humans.

That's a bold statement. But then again, I see the horrors of human nature and read books, wondering if it's true.

"You live here?" I ask her.

She shakes her head no. "We can leave. Believe it or not, you're not a prisoner here. We can come and go, but choose to stay because our mates love us, and treat us better than humans."

She gestures around and I see that the cave

surrounds a body of water. I watch as green fish men, Deep Ones, jump in and out, splash water around, drop fish on the edges. A couple women pick up the fish and start cleaning them, like it's normal for them. I watch one or two Deep Ones find women and I guess kiss them in their own way. One woman pulls another man inside one of the rooms and Celina giggles.

"It's the big dicks they have," she giggles, and I nearly choke on air. I mean, yeah, Niall has a bigger cock than before. And yes, it felt so good. And when his webbed hand rubbed my clit as Dagon fucked me almost makes me come just thinking about it.

"And Dagon?" I ask her hesitantly.

She points to a seat. "If he fucked you, then you're special. None of us have ever been with him. He brought us here and we would be dead if it wasn't for our mates. He must see something in you. And before you think we're brainwashed, no, we're not. It's hard to get past the looks at first. But it's the way they treat us, touch us. And how they take care of us." She holds up her hand with a big rock on her finger. "My mate brought me treasure from the deep. At first, I was so scared of him, even though his touch would heat my body, but he kept trying. He would bring gold pieces every day, leaving them to me as presents. Eventually he found this for me. He understands what the circle means, and I've never taken it off. We take the gold and sell it on antique websites. I made enough to pay a year of rent."

"So, you stay here to be close to your chosen one?" I ask, still trying to grasp all this. My head snaps up as the moans of the one monster and woman get loud.

"Get used to that," Celina laughs, "but yes, we choose to be here. I still have my apartment; I even have a part time job. I don't need one by any means, not when the Deep Ones bring us gems and gold to sell. That's how they've helped towns like Innswick. But the towns-people take it too far by killing people. Like I said, we were sacrifices, which sometimes become Dagon's food. But Deep Ones took to us and here we are, waiting until the next one to join us, and here *you* are. Though Dagon hasn't been happy with Innswick and the treatment of people. Other towns that have pros-pered due to the Deep Ones prosper and open up to tourists and outsiders. Innswick is one the only ones that hates outsiders."

"Which is why I'm here," I add. "I'm still grasping this. I feel like I should just run. But something tells me that it wouldn't help me, and on the other hand I feel safe here. My question is, how do you communicate with them?"

She laughs. "Somehow, you'll figure that out on your own. This is going to seem crazy."

I interrupt her. "This is all crazy."

She nods. "I agree. With my mate, it's almost like I can hear his thoughts in my head, and he can hear mine."

"Like mind reading?"

"Yeah," she says as another woman, the one that we just heard having sex, plops down in a seat next to Celina. She grabs an apple from the bowl on the table as another woman sets mugs of steaming coffee down.

"Lexi, this is Sadie." She points at the loud woman who looks like she was just thoroughly fucked, which she was, we could all hear it. "And this is May."

I wave my hand. "Hi."

I'm about to ask about how they cook and all that when the water churns and on instinct I shrink down. The women grab their coffee like they know what's coming. I know who's coming, but I'm still not prepared.

He rises from the water and beckons me. On instinct, I move toward him as the women giggle. And Celina was right, I can hear his thoughts. He's speaking to me.

"Right here?" I say out loud and his eel-like head nods. I feel webbed hands on me, and I sigh; Niall is here. I turn back to Dagon and in an instant the clothes I put on are ripped off in a roar. Niall picks me up and, right there in front of everyone, Dagon thrusts into me. I don't know if it's him, or Niall, or the fact that people are watching but I'm on fire, the need for more taking over.

"Oh, God," I moan, probably too loudly, but it doesn't matter, everyone and their mother can see what's going on. Dagon thrusts in and out as webbed hands run down the front of my body, causing goose bumps to form all over my body. I turn my head and reach up to touch Niall's face, his blue eyes shining. I feel myself getting closer and closer to coming, so close to peaking. Dagon twists his body, and I squirt—yes, I literally squirt—all over, screaming as I come undone.

Niall's tongue flicks across my cheek and then I'm gently placed on the cave floor, Dagon's hand cupping my other cheek. I reach up and grab his hand, letting him know I'm okay, just tired now. He grunts, licks my cheek in his form of a kiss, and he sinks back into the ocean. Niall waves at someone and Celina appears with a new set of clothes. Upon seeing her, I now try to cover myself, blushing at what just happened.

"Don't be upset. That was hot." She grins, helping me hide some of my dignity. Niall licks my cheek and then places a coin in my hand. A token.

Celina witnesses it and smirks at me. "See." Yeah, I see it now. He took care of me when he was human and he's still trying to do so. I'm still not sure how this all works. Will they fight over me? Or are they sharing me?

Sharing.

The thought comes into my mind and it's in Niall's old voice. I turn to him, letting him know I'm still not sure what to think of all of this.

You will. Eat.

Celina takes my hand and leads me back to the table where there are eggs, bacon, biscuits, gravy and the works waiting.

I look down at my plate, unsure of what I'm supposed to say after that. I guess Sadie is going to break the ice for me. "And I thought I was loud."

Everyone, including me, laughs. Celina introduces me to the other women, and we eat, talk about human things. May hands me another cup of coffee and I give her a grateful smile as she winks at me.

"Does that happen often?" I ask the others, and they all shake their heads.

"You're Dagon's first," Freida, a woman in her fifties, explains. From the introductions, she was the first one to be taken by one of the Deep Ones.

Should I feel special?

You are special.

An unfamiliar voice in my head says that and I turn to look over my shoulder to see Dagon lounging on the cave floor, his tail flicking in the water. If a snake, eel, or fish could smirk, he would be doing it.

"You'll get used to everything," Sadie says as I turn back to my plate. Will I?

"How do you guys cook down here?" I ask, changing the subject. May looks happy to tell me.

She points to a room. "We have electricity and with some of the coins we bought a stove, fridge, sink, the works. It's a full kitchen."

Celina chimes in, "May's the resident cook. If you want any snacks at the store, let her know." A coin drops on the table and a tail flicks it at May.

Celina and Sadie giggle as May picks it up, saying, "I guess he's pitching in for you."

Again, I should be running for the hills, but something tells me I'm right where I belong.

I stand from my seat and smile. "If you'll excuse me, I have to go pay my dues."

All the women laugh as I head for Dagon, Niall finding his way to me.

And in front of all the women, I let both men take me—several times.

When I'm totally worn out, webbed arms, strong, carry me to my bed. But I don't let Niall get far. "Your turn."

With a care one of his size couldn't possess, he pushes my legs up and slides his cock in, slowly thrusting in and out, building up my orgasm. But he knows I've already had one the minute he pushed inside. It must be something about him that makes me come on contact or thought.

He takes his web hand and slowly runs it over my clit as I moan, chasing another high. When I come again, his thrusts become faster, harder and then a few minutes later, he's croaking away as he comes.

I fall asleep in his arms, happy, despite everything.

EPILOGUE

THREE YEARS LATER

LEXI

"Push, Lexi, push," Dianne, the resident doctor, encourages me. She came to us last year and, even though she's still not accepting everything yet, she's getting there. And we're glad she's an actual doctor.

I've been here for three years now and it's been the happiest I've been, though I keep going through clothes because one of my mates likes to rip them off. I've been sleeping naked ever since we built a room closer to the front of the cave, so Dagon has easy access to me. Niall makes love to me every night, then leaves to his underground city. No one knows or can pronounce it, but from what I understand, it's where all the Deep Ones live, even little ones.

I can't tell you who the father of this little one is going to be and it's the first in the cave. Why am I giving birth here instead of in a hospital? The two reasons are at the edge of the room. Dagon's lying on the cave floor watching, his tail sometimes reaching out to comfort me. Niall is kneeling on the floor next to my bed.

Soon, wails fill the room, and I cry in relief. Dianne cleans him up and Celina wraps it in a blanket before handing the bundle to me. "It's a boy."

I nearly sob and Dagon looks at me with pride. Opening the blanket, I can see it's a human child, but that will change. And we'll be ready when the time comes. He will have two daddies who will help with the transition.

Celina rubs her stomach. "I need to go eat, mine is kicking. Want me to take him?" Celina is pregnant and I'm happy our children will only be months apart.

I glance up at Dagon and nod. "I'll come get him after."

She laughs as the other women file out. "Take your time."

As soon as they leave, Dagon pounces. He parts my legs, and his tongue lashes out, tasting everything that just came out of me. I tell them I'm a little sore and they both respond that this is only about their mate. They take turns licking my pussy, making me come several times before I can't take it anymore.

Dagon licks my lips and nods his head, off to find treasure for the baby no doubt.

Niall does a human gesture and cleans me up with a wet towel, then helps me dress. I'm a little wobbly on my feet but he hears my stomach growl. With a yelp, he picks me up, stomping toward the dining room.

He gently sets me down in a chair and nods at the women before diving back into the water. Celina is rocking my boy in a cradle and May sets a plate of food in front of me. "Eat, you'll need it."

I laugh as I gobble down the food, knowing she's right. I'm a mother now, my baby needs me. My monsters need me.

"And not just for my baby," I giggle, and everyone joins in.

Do I live a conventional life? No. Am I happy? Yes.

I didn't think I would ever be able to. I actually thought I was going crazy even after a year of great sex. But I am happy. I love both of my monsters, and they love me.

And now there will be new life to nurture, love, and prepare for the life they are going to live.

Dagon ripples the water, and I smile at the others before stripping. If I don't, he'll rip them off and I can't keep going to the store. Right there as the others eat and coo over my son, I let my monster take me, my screams of pleasure filling the cave. Yes, I'm happy.

TO EMBRACE THE ABYSS

K.C. BORDERS

"Please, make it stop!"

I gaze down at the female, her body marred and her mind shattered from my tests. For a moment, something stirs in my heart. *Pity.* Though it is not because I truly cared for her, but because I had been so hopeful she would last. *She'd shown so much promise...*

I'm ready to end her suffering when her screams suddenly escalate, a haunting crescendo that fills the air and sets my teeth on edge. With morbid fascination, I watch as blood vessels burst within the whites of her eyes. She claws at her face, in a last desperate—human —attempt to stave off her inevitable demise. Pain is etched on her contorted face, and with a final scream her body crumples to the floor. *Another one. Dead.*

I am not entirely devoid of compassion; I harbor a profound admiration for humans and the chaos they can unleash, I'm just numb to their deaths. My mere presence has driven some to madness, causing them to behave in ways that belie who they are on the outside. Their true nature is amplified in my presence.

I bore witness to the birth of humanity. Watched as countless civilizations rose and fell, saw them crumble into dust to be reborn anew from the ashes, only to build their cities upon the bones of their predecessors.

Humans are a fascinating species. Ever reaching for the divine, yearning to touch the light of the heavens, whether it be the sun or the stars. They worship anything they perceive as looming higher and larger than themselves, anything beyond their comprehension. The sun, the sky, the very earth beneath their feet.

Even a solitary man, executed on a cross, is revered for reasons they believe serve them. For some, it is merely an excuse for them to do as they wish, to sin and then seek forgiveness afterwards. It's a means to an end, allowing them to indulge in their basest desires. *They'll believe whatever they're told as long as it fits their agendas.* Others simply cling desperately to anything that might grant them purpose. *A reason for their existence...*

As a messenger, I've dutifully reported my findings on humanity back to the Outer Gods, though I've kept these experiments to myself. The less the Outer Gods know of my direct influence, the better. This world is my domain, and I like to keep some things to myself. I spread chaos among the humans in the way that a human child might pour water on an anthill. To the ants, it was either an act of nature, or the will of their gods. I've kept myself hidden in plain sight. Imagine if they knew what I truly was. The chaos would be beautiful, but it would be their end as well, with a simple snap of my fingers...

Looking upon the lifeless form of the human girl I once held such high hopes for, a grimace of distaste twists my currently human lips. I have grown weary of these futile experiments. Humans are so exquisitely fragile, and it is only out of necessity that I've pretended to care. For their suffering benefits my own darker pursuits, their ultimate destruction my nourishment. I don't consume sustenance in the normal sense of the word, like these fragile creatures do. It's unnecessary. My hunger is much deeper, more...*transcendent*. I exist to unravel minds, to tear away the thin veil of the sanity they cling to. Fear, madness, chaos; these are what sustain me in a world so perfectly chaotic. The quiver in their breath, the break in their thoughts, the way their minds shatter when they finally understand their insignificance...*that's* when I'm truly nourished. Each moment of their torment fills me, strengthens me. I take pleasure in their unraveling. They, and the chaos they breed, is my sustenance.

Though I still hope for the one that will survive… *The one perfect female.*

Long ago, I befriended and cared for a human girl. She was innocent, kind…*and blind.* She was oblivious to the truth, to the shadows that lurked within me. And so she did not fear me, even in my true form. I even allowed her delicate hands to explore one of my many forms. How her fingers traced the contours of my monstrous shape, committing every detail to memory, was a testament to her unwavering spirit. She was so blissfully unaware, untouched by the horror of my existence, and something in me always longed for such an intimate connection.

To be known by someone without their immediate destruction.

I could have granted her the gift of sight, yet I chose to let her remain blind. I understood that revealing my true self would shatter her fragile psyche. One gaze into the abyss of my eyes would have irrevocably destroyed her.

As our bond deepened, the notion of intimacy arose, an idea she expressed with great fervor. Initially I resisted, but curiosity gnawed at me, awakening desires I never knew, that I didn't even recognize, especially when it came to humans. I had never perceived them as potential mates until she unveiled that possibility.

It is not as though I've never experienced lust before. There are females in the cosmos, though they are rare and none could hold my attention for long. Most were too mindless or dull to engage in meaningful conversation; they were...*boring*. I mated only once with my own kind, and it was in my truest form. Communication was limited, as she was reticent and didn't feel the need for it. Her only intent was to mindlessly mate, to have offspring. We weren't compatible.

It was not the same with the human female. Though restraint was a concept foreign to me then, and tragically, she did not survive my passions.

I endeavored to be gentle, but as desire consumed me, I lost control. In the aftermath, I realized she perished at some point during our coupling. With her life extinguished, I felt an ache I could not ignore. I never thought I would mourn the loss of a human, but I did so, in my own way.

My grief is what began my experiments. I have indulged in the pleasures of others, engaging with multiple partners across the cosmos, all the way to its furthest reaches. Carrying a newfound spark inside of me, I began seeking out other beings that could carry an intelligent conversation and offer companionship just as the human girl had… Yet each time I sought my own release, they too succumbed to death.

It quickly became clear I needed a new approach.

Across every plane of existence, I would select small villages, nurturing them like seeds in fertile soil, and awaiting the birth of the one destined to satisfy my now insatiable appetites.

The centuries stretched before me, an eternity to most, but a blink of an eye to me. I knew it would take time for one of my stature to evolve. So, to pass the time, I allowed humans to willingly offer me worship. Sacrifices were tossed into the abyss. Some even came willingly, seeking the tantalizing thrill of surrendering to the darkness, fully aware it would lead to their doom. It was exhilarating yet exhausting, maintaining such contact. So I visited them only once every century, stirring the pot, seeking out the one who might awaken to be mine.

When weariness of waiting threatened to overtake the thrill of my quest, I took a more hands-on role, and concealed myself among the humans once again, as they were by far my favorite species. I adopted a myriad of human forms, each a mask for the monstrous power that lay beneath. I grew, not only in strength but also in wealth, weaving a tapestry of worship that ensnared the masses.

Once, I was even a pharaoh, and enjoyed spreading madness among the humans… It amused me. Over the next few centuries, I watched as they spread like wild-fire, even reaching out to the stars, yet still, no female approached the perfection I sought.

Before long, I chose a specific family that showed great promise. Every once in a while, one among them would be born who would show whispers of my influence, but each one was ultimately driven mad by their own chaos.

My mate would have to be a paradox…resilient yet malleable, strong in mind, body, and spirit, but able to be bent to my will.

The search continues still, and I shall not rest until I find her.

CHAPTER TWO

LILA

55 YEARS LATER

"Freak!" Lisa yells out as she slaps me across the face. I can barely see them through my hair, especially in this dimly lit alleyway. But I can still feel their eyes on me. When I do nothing to react, she pushes me to the ground, and I sprawl out into a muddy puddle on the asphalt. The taste of copper fills my mouth when my face connects with the ground. But I don't make a sound. I don't give them the satisfaction I know they crave. Even as her friends join in, kicking me in the stomach and various other places, I don't react.

No. I welcome the pain. Relish it. I chase the high of that feeling until it leaves me open and raw. *Maybe I'm just a super masochist?* I always tend to spark violence. Violence I cause with my mouth. With my mere existence. I don't make friends. I make enemies wherever I go. I don't know why it happens, but I've embraced it. I used to try to talk myself out of situations, but people will find anything to be angry at. A casual glance. An accidental bump of the shoulder as I walk by. So I finally started inciting it on purpose to get it over with. I don't know what my end game is.

Do I want to die?

I've always known I was different. There's something about me that makes people act crazy, and as a result I've endured a lot. My pain tolerance has always been so much higher than those around me, and it showed early on. My parents, foster parents, people in the orphanage. It didn't matter who, something in me draws out the worst in everyone, and they go off on me. But I welcome it; without the pain life feels trivial. The first time I broke a bone, I didn't cry. *I smiled.* I smiled because it was like an itch, something deep within finally being scratched. It felt good. But that feeling never lasted long enough.

I even heal faster than most. It's not instantaneous, I'm not Wolverine, but it's still pretty quick. While it may take weeks or months for most to heal from a compound fracture, it only takes me about half the time, and that time frame is getting shorter. The more I break, the faster I heal, the more I come alive.

"Careful, you might actually kill the little dog shit," Lisa says with a laugh as she sits back, watching me get the shit kicked out of me. They finally stop, all standing back and panting, tired from their efforts. I get my palms and knees under me, raising myself up. Blood drips into the dirt under my broken nose, the tiny puddles coalescing together to form a larger one.

"Eww, gross." Lisa moves back over to me and places her dirty black boot on the side of my head, shoving me back to the ground. I feel the biting sting of the asphalt as it rips into my flesh, and Lisa crouches over me. "You should stay the fuck down, Freak. You'll only piss me off."

Freak. My favorite word. If they only knew.

"Why won't you scream? Or talk? Did we actually break you this time?" Blake asks from behind her, his arms folded over his chest as his gaze rakes over me with an all too familiar hunger in his eyes, one I've seen far too many times...

I realize my skirt is hiked up, and press it down. "You wish," I sneer, quickly lifting my head and spitting blood in Lisa's face. She's the closest to me, so she gets the first dose of my retaliation. Lisa shrieks and stumbles back as she attempts to wipe it off. Her cronies immediately resume stomping on and kicking me. I feel a rib crack and I almost moan in pleasure. I don't understand it, don't know why I'm like this, but pain is everything. Pain makes me feel *something*. It lets me know I am alive. *Though I've never been beaten to near death before, so this should be a new experience.*

"You fucking bitch!" Lisa screams, and pushes her way back into the fray, just to slam her heel down into my ribs.

This time I do moan, and glare up at her with a sadistic grin. "Hurt me again! I like it!"

Lisa backs away. "You're so fucking disgusting!"

Some of the guys in the pack accept my invitation and deliver more blows to my body. My pleasure only increases with each blow, and then I feel it. A literal fucking knife in my back. I scream out a moan, an action that makes them all step back. All but Blake, who has a wild glint in his eyes. A born killer, using me for his sick fantasy. I know this because he confided in me once. He told me all about what he wanted as he raped me.

It was another time Lisa and her little band attacked me. They beat me until I was unconscious, then left me with him. I woke to him shoving his cock inside me. His hands were around my throat when he came, and he was grunting as he told me how he wondered what it would be like to kill someone. He even held the very same knife against my throat when he was done, stating how he'd love to watch me bleed out as his come leaked out of my pussy... I barely felt it though. *He wasn't my first.*

"Come on baby, do it again," I groan, daring him to retrieve the knife and stab me again. My clothes are already damp from my sweat and the filth of the street, but I can feel the blood beginning to seep from around the knife, making my shirt sticky. Blake stares down at me, wide-eyed.

"Don't stop now, pull it out and stick me again you fucking pussy!" I scream, and wait for him to follow through, but he doesn't. He leaves me wanting, like they always do. Leaving the knife in my back, he steps away. "Pussy!" I spit, shooting bloody foam in his direction before slowly picking myself up and standing upright. "Isn't anyone brave enough to fucking finish me off?" I ask as I move through them, dragging myself toward Lisa, who's still backing away.

I guess I do want to die.

"What the fuck, bitch? What are you? Are you on something or just fucking *crazy*?"

"Cut me open and let's find out. I'm just your pinata anyway." I must have bitten my tongue or something because blood is pooling in my mouth. I spit it to the side before continuing, "Let's see what makes me tick, huh?"

"You're a fucking psycho!" She steps back again. "Guys, can someone please put this dog down and let's get the fuck out of here?"

"Aww, is Lisa tired of her little punching bag? Come

on, I love our sessions. They always leave me feeling all warm and tingly inside," I sneer. "Hit me, bitch. Hit me again—" I feel a blow to the back of my head, and I instantly see stars as pain radiates through my skull. My body hits the ground hard. "Is that all you got?" My voice is distant as the ringing in my ears drowns out everything around me, it's almost peaceful. The beat of music pouring from the club near me almost matches the thrumming beat of my heart in my ears and I feel myself fading into the rhythm.

The wail of sirens pierces the night, cutting through the fog of pain as well as the music, and the euphoria that clouds my mind. Some do-gooder must have called this in, ruining my fun. The predators that encircled me scatter like roaches in the light, their bravado dissolving into fear. I remain where I am, half of my body on top of a pile of trash while the rest of me soaks up a puddle of what I hope is water on the broken asphalt. The coolness of it grounds me in this moment, as I come to terms with my life, wondering what my purpose is. What it's all for, even as the stench of rotted trash fills my senses.

The knife still protrudes from my back, a twisted trophy from my latest encounter. This will just be another scar to add to my collection. I can still taste blood as it fills my mouth, thick and metallic, mingling with the grime of the alleyway as the grit crunches between my teeth.

I wonder, briefly, if I should simply let go. End my suffering and let the darkness claim me. It would be so easy, so peaceful. I have nothing and no one, so what's the point of going on? With everything I've endured, giving up is all that is left. My own parents didn't want me, they claimed they couldn't live another day with me in their presence. And nobody has wanted me ever since.

I've endured nothing but pain my whole life. I was a sweet kid, always ready to smile even as people hurt me. But when I aged out of the orphanage, my bullies still followed me. It's like they're obsessed with their pursuits of violence against me. They know the places I frequent, that I've been trying to get a job at the club. They want to make me miserable, and it pisses me off. I've done nothing wrong, except for existing.

The thought of surrendering, of allowing the void to swallow me whole, of letting everyone else win in my fight for survival, ignites something in me. A flicker of defiance deep within. A fire that rages to life. *NO! Not yet. There's still more to endure, more to feel... If I can just get away from here, start somewhere new, maybe I'll have a chance. A chance at a real fucking life...*

Footsteps approach, heavy and purposeful, unlike the frantic retreat of my attackers. My vision blurs, but I can make out the silhouette of a dark figure, tall and imposing, moving through the shadows with an unnerving grace. Blue and red lights dance in the distance, and the sound of the ambulance grows louder as it gets closer. I force my body to obey, to rise, despite the pain that radiates from every corner of my being, but only manage to sit up on my knees. I spit out another mouthful of blood, silently daring this newcomer to try and finish what the others couldn't.

"Stay where you are," a deep, masculine voice commands, low and authoritative. There's such power within it that I almost want to obey, and I stiffen with indecision. That has me wincing as I feel a shift in the muscles around the blade, forcing it deeper and tearing them further. The figure steps into the dim light cast by a flickering street lamp, and I catch my first real glimpse of him. He's definitely tall, and dressed in a long, dark coat that seems to blend with the night itself. His face is obscured by the shadow of his fedora and I find myself straining to get a peek at him. As he slightly tilts his head at me his eyes become visible, and seem to glow. *A trick of the streetlight?* They are a sharp icy blue, cold, and calculating. It feels as if they pierce through my soul, making a chill run through me. I'm not usually scared of people, but this man's presence elicits something deep inside of me that I've never felt before...fear.

Sirens sound close by, the flashing red and blue lights reflecting off the slick pavement as they attempt to turn down the alleyway. The man in front of me pays them no mind, and he doesn't seem too fazed by my appearance either. No concern. If anything, he appears amused by the spectacle. He tilts his head again, observing me with a curiosity that makes my skin crawl. I don't bother pressing my skirt down this time, I'm too tired to care.

"Like what you see, asshole? " I manage to rasp out, my voice raw and strained. "Do you want to get a few licks in too?"

He doesn't answer immediately. Instead, he steps closer, so close that I can smell him—an intoxicating mix of leather, smoke, and something else, something I can't seem to recall. *Cognac maybe?* He reaches out, and I flinch instinctively, but he doesn't touch me. His hand hovers above the handle of the knife in my back, as if he's considering whether to remove it.

"Something like that. You should be dead, little one," he finally murmurs, his voice laced with something I can't quite place.

"Sorry to disappoint," I sneer, my words dripping with sarcasm despite the pain that shoots through my body with every breath. Normally, pain feels good, but the high sometimes wears off and leaves all of me feeling like a raw, open wound. This is one of those times.

His lips twitch into a smile, a predator's smile, revealing the whites of his teeth. The hair rises on the back of my neck and I realize with a sinking feeling that this man may be more dangerous than anyone I've ever encountered.

"Perhaps you're not so disappointing after all," he says with a smirk.

Then, with a sudden, fluid motion, he pulls the knife from my back and I fall to my hands. I bite down on a scream as white-hot pain shoots through my spine, but I don't give him the satisfaction of hearing my hurt. Instead, I regard him as another assailant, glaring up at him through a haze of agony, my vision tunneling as my body fights to remain conscious.

"What do you want?" I manage to choke out, my hands and knees threatening to buckle beneath me. My body begins to shudder and my teeth chatter uncontrollably, a response to trauma I haven't had in a long while. A reaction I've always found strange, given my propensity for pain.

He doesn't answer. Instead, he twirls the bloodied knife in his hand, inspecting it with a detached interest before casually tossing it aside. The metal pings when it hits the pavement. His eyes meet mine, and for a moment, I feel as though I'm being pulled into his gaze.

The ambulance finally pulls into the alleyway a few feet down, but stops again due to all the trash in the way. "You'll know soon enough," he finally says, his voice barely more than a whisper. Yet it sounds like a threat. All of my alarm bells go off as his words resonate in my skull like a warning. Like the sound of a bell tolling my doom. "For now, it's time for you to rest, little one. We have much to discuss when you awaken."

When I awaken?

Before I can protest, gravity takes me back to the asphalt and my vision goes black. The last thing I hear is the echo of his laughter, cold and cruel, as I slip into unconsciousness.

CHAPTER THREE

I feel weightless, as though I'm suspended in an ocean of nothingness. There's no ground beneath my feet, no sense of up or down, just...stillness. Brilliant stars stretch out in every direction, glittering, colorful pinpricks amidst the infinite black, broken apart by bursts of colorful nebulas. It's beautiful, hauntingly so, but terrifying in a way I can't fully describe. I've never truly seen anything like it, nothing compares or even comes close.

I try to breathe, but there's no air. There's no need for it. My lungs don't ache, my body doesn't struggle. It's like I'm more spirit than flesh now, and I know I must be dead, floating in this vast emptiness. Could this be purgatory? I feel small, insignificant. My mind wanders, searching for any sound, any signs of life. But there's only silence, the kind that hums and echoes with its intensity.

For a moment, it's peaceful. The quiet, the isolation, it

wraps around me like a warm blanket, comforting in its own strange way. There's no pain, no chaos. No one is screaming at me. No one is hurting me. It's as if the universe has swallowed me whole, and I'm drifting in its belly, untouched by time or fear or violence. But then the loneliness sets in. It crawls up from the pit of my stomach, like a gnawing ache that grows with every heartbeat. Part of me wanted to die, but I wasn't ready. What I really wanted was to find my place in the world. I wanted to feel joy. To feel love. To be... loved. I wanted to marry a good man who was kind and would treat me well.

As I weep for the fool that I was, I reach out, but there's nothing to touch. No one to hold onto. It's as though I'm the only being left, suspended between worlds, forgotten like the nothing that I am. That I... was. The stars twinkle back at me, distant and indifferent. I regard them as beings that don't care about my insignificance. They've been here since long before me, and they'll be here long after I fade away.

Two stars of blue come together as eyes, floating in the vastness. Eyes that watch me with expressed interest. It's then I feel heat flood my body, and I become all too aware of my own naked skin. Silhouettes and tentacled shadows that seem to be attached to a shrouded figure stand out against the colorful backdrop, moving of their own accord. The long, snake-like appendages wrap around me and spread my legs. My brain is in a fog as a sensation, unlike anything I've ever felt, comes over me. The being seems to tease at my entrance before entering me. One of the strange appendages slides with ease, in and out, stretching me as it probes deeply.

I find my voice among the stars, hear myself moaning as I come undone, gasping as I am quickly brought to a sweet release. The entity leaves me, as quickly as it appeared, and I'm alone once more.

My body feels cold for a while, and I long for its return. In this crushing solitude, there's a strange sort of calm. Like being cradled by the abyss itself, held gently by the vastness of the cosmos. There's no pressure, no expectations. I simply exist, floating endlessly in a place where nothing and every-thing collide, creating explosions of beauty and mystery. For the first time in my life, I know what peace feels like and I wonder if I imagined the creature.

I startle awake, mentally cursing at the wet dream as the scent of antiseptic fills my nostrils. And instead of the cold, dirty alley, I'm greeted by a soft, warm light. The sounds of machines beeping are still distant, drowned out by the pounding in my head. My body feels like it's made of lead, each breath a reminder of the pain coursing through me. When I finally take stock of my surroundings, I realize I'm in a luxurious room, almost suite-like, with plush bedding draped in silk sheets that feel cool against my skin. A vase of fresh lilies sits on the bedside table, their fragrance soothing. But then I notice the metal bars on my bed and the IV in my arm. My fuzzy head falls back onto the pillow, and I let out a sigh as the quick action makes my vision spin. *I'm in a hospital.*

Panic grips me for a moment. Where am I? How did I get here? And then I remember the ambulance. As I try to sit up, a sharp pain shoots through my back and ribs, reminding me of what happened. I wince, falling back against the pillows once more, and I assume I must have been hurt more than I realized. That's when I notice them. Gifts. I don't know how I missed them.

Lavish, extravagant gifts surround me. Boxes wrapped in gold paper, tied with delicate white ribbons. A bottle of expensive champagne. A set of diamonds glinting from a red velvet case sitting next to me on the bedside table. This isn't just a hospital, it's a dream. *Someone else's dream.* Because who would bring me here? Who would leave these gifts? *Surely they have the wrong person. They can't be for me.*

A soft knock on the door pulls me from my thoughts. A slender woman with blonde hair and purple scrubs enters the room, her movements graceful and efficient. "Oh, you're awake. Good morning, Miss Morgan," she says with a warm smile as she points at her nametag. "I'm nurse Jenna. How are you feeling?" Her smile doesn't feel genuine. It feels…*forced.*

"I—I'm fine," I manage to say, though I'm not sure that it's true. "Where am I? How do you know who I am?"

I see her beginning to tense up. Something everyone

does around me. "You're in a private facility," she explains, checking the IV attached to my arm. "You were brought here for treatment after your injuries. Everything is taken care of."

"By whom?" I ask, my voice shaky. "Who brought me here, and how do you know who I am?" I ask again.

"Lila," she says softly, turning to face me again, ignoring my questions. Her expression is a mixture of both concern and awe. "You're lucky to be alive. What you went through should've killed you. You have extensive injuries, and a major concussion, but...you're healing remarkably fast. Faster than anything I've ever seen."

I blink, trying to process her words through the haze of confusion. *Am I healing faster than I normally do?* I shift uncomfortably under her scrutiny. *She's going to find out that I'm a freak, and not some miracle.* "Can you answer my questions? Who brought me here, and how do you know my name?"

The nurse hesitates for a moment, then smiles again. "Your benefactor prefers to remain anonymous for now. But he's made sure you have everything you need. He's the one who told us who you are."

I stare at her, trying to process what she's saying. *An anonymous benefactor? Who the hell would do this for me and how does he know me? I don't know anyone who would do something like this for me.*

Before I can ask more questions, she's already

heading for the door. "Just rest, Miss Morgan," she says before leaving the room. "You're safe here."

Safe. The word echoes in my mind as I look around the room again. Whoever this benefactor is, they've spared no expense. But why? Why go to all this trouble for someone like me? *A nobody.*

I sink back into the pillows yet again, my thoughts racing. With the high gone, the pain in my back throbs, but it's nothing compared to the confusion swirling in my head. Obviously, whatever pain relief they have me on isn't doing the trick. *Not that I mind it.* I look around the room again and stare in awe. *These gifts can't be for nothing.* I'm not used to all this luxury, care, or attention. All my life, I've been kicked down, broken, and left to pick up the pieces on my own. *Why now? Why me?*

As the questions pile up, exhaustion pulls at me. My eyes grow heavy despite the whirlwind in my mind, and as sleep takes over, I wonder if the nurse put something in my IV.

~CB~

When I wake again, the sun has shifted, casting a golden glow over the room. A soft rustling catches my attention, and when my eyes adjust, I see him…The figure of a man. I assume the same one from the alley. He's tall and impeccably dressed, standing by the window with his back to me. His form casts a shadow that seems to stretch across the room, reaching my bed. He's watching the world outside, but I can feel his presence filling the room.

"Good morning," he almost purrs, his voice deep and alluring.

"Who are you?" My voice is rough, but the question clearly demands an answer.

He turns slowly, and crosses the room to stand beside me. The first thing I notice are those eyes—piercing blue that seem to be filled with a dark intensity as well as something I can't discern, and I'm reminded of my dream. *Those eyes.* I have to tear myself away from his amused gaze to survey the rest of him. His features are sharp, handsome in a way that's almost otherworldly. His suit is tailored to perfection and screams high class money. He looks like he stepped out of an issue of *GQ*. This is a man who commands power, exudes confidence, and takes what he wants. *Mafia maybe?*

"I'm the one who saved you," he says, his voice deep, and smooth as velvet. "The one who brought you here."

"Why?" The questions tumble out before I can stop them. "Why go to all this trouble for a stranger?" *The EMTs didn't bring me here? The last thing I remember is his strange laughter as he walked away, leaving me behind...*

He takes a step closer, and I can feel the air change around us, charged with something I don't understand. "Because you're someone of great interest to me, Lila," he says, and the way he speaks my name sends a shiver down my spine.

I have to hold in a scoff. I don't want to be rude to my benefactor. "You're the one who brought me? The last thing I remember is you walking away, laughing at me like an idiot." I wince at myself, not meaning to say that last part, but I couldn't help myself. I'm used to staying on the defensive and I know nothing comes free. "You don't know me. There's nothing special or interesting about me, so why help me?" I glare as he reaches out, taking the gifts from the chair to set them on the ground. *Why the gifts? Why did he help me?*

The man takes a seat in the chair near me, cutting my thoughts short as he leans on the sidebar of my bed. His intoxicating scent swirls around me. "You're wrong, Lila."

The sound of my name skates across my skin again and warmth fills my core, making it clench. A reaction that frankly startles me. No one turns me on. *No one.* I can't describe the strange attraction I suddenly feel to him, even as I can sense the danger lurking in him and see it reflected in the depths of his cold blue eyes. *Maybe it's the danger I'm attracted to?* "How can you be so sure? Who are you?"

The man's lips curve into a soft; unsettling smile. "That would take too long to explain. For now, call me... Nyler."

"Nyler? That's an interesting name." I find myself

staring at him. Captivated by the way he moves, how graceful and precise he is, and I realize he's watching me too.

He stares at me for a long moment, before something in his gaze flickers and becomes darker. I notice the look of desire in his eyes, the same look I've seen before in others. But the reaction my body has to him is visceral. My core clenches again at the idea of him standing over me, my legs spread, waiting for him to take me. *What the hell is wrong with me?*

I shake my head and gasp at the intrusive thoughts that are so unlike me. The smirk on Nyler's face deepens. "Are you alright, Lila? The expressions on your face tell me you are confused," he says, like he knows he's affecting me.

I try to keep the conversation on point, while also trying to ignore my arousal. "There was an ambulance coming down the alleyway–"

"I had them bring you here, so you're closer to me."

I ignore that he's cut me off, but I can't ignore the implications of his words, or the fear they draw out. "Closer to you, why?" I sigh, feeling aggravated and a little creeped out. "Again, I don't know you; why would you want me closer to you?" I pull the covers up to my chest as if the thin fabric could offer me any protection. "Is this a sex thing?"

Nyler leans in closer with a dark chuckle. "Is that what you want, Lila? Don't you want to get to know me first?" He grins, and I feel myself blush for the first time in forever. This man is playing me like a fiddle, speaking directly to the butterflies in my stomach.

"I-I… That's not what I meant," I stammer out, feeling anger rise. "What is this all about? And why the lavish gifts? Don't you think they're over the top?"

"You," Nyler says simply. "It's all about you."

My eyes roll, and I let out a breathy sigh as I lay back against the pillow.

Nyler reaches out to my cloth-covered thigh and I flinch, watching him warily. He smirks as his fingertips graze the fabric before lifting something with a cord. I watch as he presses a button, and my bed lifts at the head, forcing me to sit up and face him.

My jaw hangs open and a small smile tugs at the corners of my lips before I quickly wipe it away. I don't understand his brazen attitude, like he owns everything. Then I remember he's probably paying for everything. *It's not my bed. It's his.* My core tightens again when he lays the remote back down on my thigh. His hand lingers for a moment too long as he gently strokes the fabric before he pulls it away. The spot feels cold with the sudden absence of his touch. I'm used to unwanted contact, but I'm not used to wanting contact. There was something about the way he touched me. It was almost comforting. In that moment, I felt the chaos in my mind bleed away.

Nyler closes his eyes and inhales through his nose.

"You're incredible, Lila." He says, his lids lifting to gaze at me. "I've waited so long for you."

"What do you mean?" *Another red flag. And there were already so many. This dude must be a creep. A rich, disgustingly handsome creep...*

"So many questions." He shifts in his seat before standing and I watch as he grips the bars of my bed, leaning into my space.

He's so close, I can feel the warmth of his body and once again smell his unique scent of leather, smoke, and cognac. It wraps around me like an embrace, and I close my eyes for a moment, not wanting to get lost in the depths of his icy gaze.

"Look at me, Lila." His voice slides over me. It's too seductive. Too alluring.

I hesitate at first, forcing myself not to look, but I find my head turning involuntarily to face him. It's like I can't help myself, and when I'm caught by his piercing blues I can't look away. They're beautiful, full of darkness, desire, and promise… Turbulent like the sea. *Pure chaos.*

"What do you feel right now, Lila?" He pauses. "And please…be precise. Do you feel your mind spiraling, or slipping?"

"Spiral—slipping?" My brows furrow in confusion. "No. I feel…" I pause, wondering why I'm answering him as I consider what I'm actually feeling. *What DO I feel? There's a sense of…calmness. Yes, I'm calm. Despite this bizarre event, I don't feel as frightened as I was.* "I feel calm, mostly." I finally answered.

Nyler's eyes flicker with a glint of excitement. His hand reaches out to me, and before I can attempt to move—with nowhere to go anyway, his hand slips behind my back, and he leans in to wrap his arms around me. My body becomes rigid under his touch, my mind clouding further with confusion.

"What–"

"Shhh. Just give me a moment, please, Lila."

His warmth seems to permeate my body. I honestly can't remember the last time someone hugged me, or showed me any real affection, and I wonder if he's doing it for me. My emotions swirl, threatening to spill over. Tears sting at my eyes, but I tamp them down, clearing my throat. "Okay, buddy. I think that's enough."

"Nyler, please," he says, pulling back. "You really are a marvel, Lila. You're destined for great things."

"Nyler—" I start, but pause when he smiles suddenly.

"Yes?"

"Could you get the nurse? I would like to leave now. I feel fine."

Nylar's gaze scans over me. "You've only been here for two days and you feel okay?"

"There's pain, but it's manageable. I don't mind it." I wince after I say it, realizing how it must sound.

His brow lifts. "Do you have anywhere to go once you leave?"

I hesitate, but nod, wondering if he already knows the truth. "Yeah, a few places–"

"No. I thought not," he cuts me off, as if he read my mind. "I have a spare room. You'll stay with me, below my club.

"Your club?"

He nods.

"Then you're not some sort of mob boss?"

He's quick to grin. "Mob bosses can't have clubs?"

"Oh, I mean… I guess they can have whatever they want."

"I want you, Lila."

CHAPTER FOUR

My core instantly clenches and I feel my cheeks flush. I try to ignore his last statement, not taking any real stock in it because it doesn't make any sense. "So, that's a yes? You're in the mob?"

Nyler leans into my space, and I feel the heat of his breath feather against my ear as he whispers. "Mafia."

Chills erupt across my skin, and the gasp that leaves me has him grinning wider. He leans back and reaches out to touch my chin, lifting it to close my jaw as he stares down into my eyes. "Rent is free. Water is free. Food is free. I'll even take you on a shopping spree. You can have whatever you desire."

"What's the catch?"

"You. That's it. Nothing else."

"What do you mean?"

"You'll be mine, Lila. You'll do what I say, when I say, and you won't complain."

My jaw drops again. *The nerve of this man. Who does he think he is? So he wants an obedient sex doll?*

"We'll get to know each other much better there. We'll have privacy. You can tell me all about your hopes and dreams."

"Nyler," I start again. *No one has ever asked me what my hopes and dreams are...*

At the mention of his name, his smile deepens once more, and it catches me off guard. "Yes, Lila?"

"I don't understand any of this. I don't know you. You don't know me. Why would I ever go with you? What exactly is this?"

"The start of something beautiful and otherworldly."

My brows furrow. "I'm going to ask you again. Is this a sex thing? Or am I going to wake up in your basement missing organs?"

His dark chuckle has me blushing again but I don't let up.

"I'm serious, Nyler. I want to know what your plans are for me. You clearly have something in mind." *Oh god, is he going to experiment on me? Dissect me because of my healing abilities?*

Nyler continues to hover over me. "I need a companion, Lila. And there is no other. There is only you. In exchange, I can give you everything you've never had."

I search his gaze. This whole thing feels like it's straight out of a movie, like it's simply too good to be true. "Like love?" I test.

His gaze heats. "Define love."

"If you can't answer that question, then you can't offer it. Please call the nurse, I'd like to leave," I say again. Folding my arms across my chest, forcing myself to pry my eyes away from his.

"You're wrong, Lila." His voice takes on a more gentle tone, which pulls me back in. "I have a feeling you could teach me how to love. I've never experienced such a human emotion, and I've waited long enough." He pauses, tilting his head. "Are you willing to love me, Lila?"

I feel a chill rush over me yet again, and bumps prickle across my skin. *Human? What else would it be?* "That's not something I can answer right now, Nyler. At the risk of sounding like a broken record, I don't know you. This is insanity." I quickly pull the covers over my head to avoid his penetrating gaze.

"Please try to answer, Lila. We are both in need of the one thing we can only give to each other." How would he know? How could he possibly know that? After a moment, I allow myself to think about it, and I can't believe I'm actually considering it.

At one point, I was so ready to throw my life away without ever experiencing such a thing. But with a complete stranger? It's not like I—wait... He hasn't tried to hurt me yet.

He hasn't screamed at me. He's never once seemed uncomfortable around me. I think this is the longest I've ever spent in someone's presence that hasn't tried to inflict harm on me. Maybe he won't be like everyone else.

"I'll do it," I answer suddenly, feeling a tremor run through my body as if I were staring down the barrel of a gun. Dark ribbons of shadows seem to dance beyond the sheet, and I assume it's Nyler moving about. Though I'm yet again reminded of the dream, remembering the dark appendages and the way they wrapped around me....

I feel the weight of the sheet covering me shift as he slowly pulls it down and captures me with his gaze again. The look in his eyes is so primal it almost shocks me. "You'll do what, Lila? I need to hear it."

"I—I'll be yours." I shudder, feeling like I sold my soul to the devil. *But what did I have to lose?*

Nyler smiles, flashing his pearly whites. "Do you promise?"

I nod slowly, and his smile deepens.

His hand lifts to gently brush the hair from my face, a gesture I've never actually experienced, and only ever seen in movies. His touch sends a thrill through me, amping up my strange arousal. "Good girl," he says, his voice smooth and panty melting. He moves his hand slowly, dragging it along the side of my cheek before allowing it to slide down my arm. His gentle touch moves to my thigh, and I tense, feeling my core clench.

I feel him pluck the remote from my leg again, and watch as he presses a button.

There's a ping. "Yes? Can I help you?" A nurse's voice comes through the intercom with notes of static.

"Miss Morgan would like to inquire about her immediate departure." Nyler's gaze never leaves mine. I see the desire there, and it frightens me. *He feels like a predator that's just waiting to strike. What exactly did I agree to? I'm not ready to become a lab rat or someone's plaything. No matter how tempting he is. And yet...I want him.* As I stare into his eyes, I find my reasons for denying him slipping away, and I feel like I just want to submit to him.

"Oh, alright. I'll send someone to check her vitals and let the doctor know."

"Thank you, Nurse." He lays the remote back onto my thigh, and leans into my space once again.

"Of course." The intercom clicks, breaking my connection with Nyler's gaze.

"If I go with you, what will be expected of me?" I purse my lips together, nervously chewing on my bottom lip and drawing his eyes to the movement.

"There is no 'If', Lila." He reaches out and tilts my head as he looks me in the eyes. "You've already agreed. But I expect you not to run, no matter what you see, or how you feel."

· · ·

Alarm bells rise again. "What exactly does that mean? Do I no longer have the choice to leave? And what would I see—murder? Do you kill people, Mr. Mafia Man?"

His smirk is slow. "Well, you'd be going against your word if you back out. You're mine, Lila. You belong to me now. Maybe it would ease your worries were you to experience a sample of what I have to offer you?"

"You didn't answer my question," I say bluntly.

He grins. "I'll answer you, after you answer me."

"Okay, fine. Sure. Show me what you have to offer."

His grin is almost wicked, but I'm willing to play his game. "Go for it."

Nyler's hand quickly dips under the blanket and slides across my thigh. His digits connect with my core and I gasp at the sudden intrusion. It's then that I realize I'm not wearing any underwear. His fingers suddenly feel boneless, and longer than humanly possible as they slowly enter me. Not one, but several seem to *slither* along my mound and delve within me. Each finger-like appendage seems to pulse with a life of its own, and I feel myself losing my grip on reality as ecstasy immediately fills every fiber of my being. He strokes mercilessly at my sensitive nub as two or more of his fingers explore deeper. I finally let out a moan, gripping the sides of the bed rails, my head spinning as I orgasm.

"I do, in fact, kill people," he admits as I feel another

finger slide to my anus, entering me deeply and without warning. The intrusion forces a moment of stark clarity, and I realize… he's not human.

What his hand is doing to me, isn't normal at all. It's not possible, but it brings me to heights I've never felt. I come again, harder than before, and cry out my release. When I open my eyes again, his hand is gone and he's standing near the window as if nothing has happened, an amused look on his face.

Nyler crosses the room and smirks. "Lila? Are you okay? I think you passed out at my confession. Are you scared of me now, knowing I kill people?"

My jaw drops for the billionth time and my face heats. *What the fuck just happend? Was that real? Did I imagine it or dream it? Is my head more damaged than I thought?* The questions pile up and I'm now at war with myself. *This is such a bizarre turn of events and I can barely wrap my head around what just happened. Or... what I think happened?*

"Lila?" he says my name again, and reaches out to close my jaw.

He's a killer. An inhuman killer. And I'm letting him have me. Why aren't I more concerned? Why am I not afraid of him? I shake my head, and he smiles. I've seen death before, plenty of it. But I've never knowingly been around a killer. Blake had only talked about killing, and I probably would have been his first victim if this man hadn't called the ambulance. Memories from that night filter in like a flashback. *The music.* "The alleyway I was in— You said you owned a club. Was I behind your club?"

Nyler nods. "Yes, Club Void."

"Okay. So I've been in your club and dropped off an application. Is that how you know my name?" *The question feels so trivial now, after the mindfuck I just experienced, and I feel like I should be asking other questions.*

Nyler starts to answer, when a knock at the door interrupts us.

"Come in," I say quickly, eager to get it over with. The nurse steps in, followed by an older gentleman in a white coat with gray hair and silver glasses.

"Good evening, Miss Morgan. I'm Doctor Michael," he starts, his glasses slipping down the bridge of his nose as he approaches and glances down at his clipboard. "I hear you're ready to leave us?" I simply nod and look away, catching sight of the nurse beside me checking my IV bag before she begins to quickly type something up on the computer. My attention turns back to the doctor, and I can tell he has more to say.

Michael glances over to Nyler briefly, giving him a curt nod, visibly uncomfortable. Nyler doesn't respond, but I can sense a tension between them. The doctor's gaze settles back on me. "Miss Morgan, your recovery has been... remarkable," he begins, his voice a little too loud, and a little too rushed as if he's in a desperate hurry. "We're still unsure of how, and we'd like to draw some blood to–"

"No," Nyler says abruptly. His eyes are locked on me though, and I have to wonder what he's thinking.

"I'm sorry sir, but I was speaking to Miss Morg–"

"I said no." With ice in his eyes, Nyler turns to Michael. "She will be leaving right now. The only thing you will be drawing are whatever papers you require for her to sign so we can be on our way. Or we'll simply cut through the red tape and walk out of here without jumping through all your little hoops."

The doctor visibly slinks backward and nods. "Right. Okay. Very well." He cuts his eyes at me. "If you ever change your mind and decide to help others–"

"I don't think you understand," Nyler interrupts smoothly, the calm in his voice making the hair on the back of my neck stand up. He's still sitting, but I can feel something shifting, like a cold draft snaking its way through the room. "I brought her here to be healed. Not to be experimented on."

The doctor's hand trembles slightly as he flips a page on the clipboard, trying to maintain his composure. He clears his throat, stammering slightly, "Of course, we—we wouldn't..."

Nyler's voice drops lower, barely above a whisper,

but it carries weight. "Then perhaps you should remember we said no. Her health is all that matters now. Nothing else. And she's ready to go, so make it happen."

"Sure, of course. We just need to make sure she's alright," he tries once more, stepping toward me. "If we could just quickly draw some blood and then–"

Nyler stands abruptly, his towering figure casting an impossibly long shadow across the doctor, and seeming to stretch along the sterile floor. I blink, surprised by the sudden movement. He doesn't *look* angry, at least, not outwardly. But something in the air shifts again. The doctor takes another step back, his eyes wide and his throat bobbing nervously.

Nyler doesn't need to speak anymore. I can almost feel the threat in the air, like some invisible force. The room feels colder, and the poor doctor's breathing is shallow. The mafia man hasn't even touched the doctor, he hasn't raised a hand or his voice… he hasn't needed to. The doctor looks paler now, more disoriented, like he's drowning in his own fear. But all I can see from my bed is Nyler standing there, composed and collected— his expression unreadable.

Without another word, the doctor hurries out, practically fleeing the room. I shake my head slightly, in shock at what just unfolded. No one has ever stood up for me before. My eyes shift to Nyler. He smirks at me, and a flicker of something darker lingers behind his gaze, though he quickly softens it with a smile. "Don't worry, Lila," he says, his voice calm and soothing, "you're with me now. I will protect you." And I want to believe him.

I feel something in me stir at his words. Something unfamiliar, or long abandoned. And I feel raw and more vulnerable than I ever have before, like I am laid bare in front of him. All I've known is pain, and this man—this stranger—has shown me more kindness than anyone in all my eighteen years of life.

I'm overwhelmed with a sense of confusion and gratitude. *Why would he do that for me? Why would he stand up for me like that?* The dam holding my tears finally breaks and I allow myself to cry. Just a little.

CHAPTER FIVE

NYLER

My eyes linger on Lila as she prepares to leave, watching her silently while she signs the discharge papers. Her sparkling emerald gaze glides over the parchment as she reads the terms of her release, and her slender fingers grip the pen a little too tightly. Her unease is obvious. But she's mine now. *All mine... I finally found her, and I've already given her a little nibble of what's to come.* Despite her being something more than most humans, she is still quite the fragile thing, though I know she'll never admit it.

I've seen her strength and determination, and her delicate nature coupled with that unwavering strength is what stirs something dark and primal within me. That, and the added fact that she is everything I've wanted for over a millennium. *At least, that is my deepest hope.* The way her hand trembles slightly as she signs the form, like she knows she's signing her life away, only adds to the simmering excitement coiling inside of me. She doesn't feel the crushing madness around me that others feel, as my presence pulls and tears at the edges of their minds, threatening to unravel their sanity. No. She said she feels...*calm. A new and exciting development. An absolute first for me.*

She has no idea what truly awaits her once we leave this hospital. No notion of the way I will bend and test her once I have her within my home, in my domain, within my grasp; where every shadow obeys, and she will have no choice but to do the same. When she was focused on the doctor, I tasted her on my fingers. Licked them clean. I had never done that before, but I couldn't contain myself. Around her, my arousal builds with each passing moment. She is like a gift that I cannot wait to unwrap and open. To exploit. To break and reshape. She thinks she's free. But soon, I will strip her of that final shred of control she clings so desperately to. *Her humanity.* Only then will she ever truly be free... Be wholly mine.

Filthy images fill my mind as I imagine her in my bed, wrapped in my silken sheets, not knowing whether the touch on her skin is real or something more. My power throbs beneath the surface, ready to rise, but I hold it in check. There's no need to rush. Patience is the key, and I will savor every second as she walks willingly into the trap I've set. I've waited this long, and I want to enjoy every second spent with her.

I can sense her exhaustion, the way her body longs for rest. True rest. But it would find none. N*ot with me, not yet*. While she was sleeping, I entered her mind and found her desires. There's a darkness in her that calls to mine. With everything she's had to endure, she's already so beautifully broken, my little *Kintsugi*, she will be so easily molded to my will. Her beauty, her resilience, it all feeds into my desires. I can already picture her at my mercy, writhing in ecstasy as her defenses crumble and she finally realizes there is no escape. I will relish that moment, that look in her eyes when she finally understands she belongs completely to me.

As she hands the clipboard back to the nurse, the corner of my lips pulls into a smile. Soon, we will leave this sterile place behind, and in the darkness of my home I will claim what is rightfully mine.

But for now, I keep my face as impassive as I can, never alluding to the dark thoughts swirling in my mind. Just as my gaze never leaves her as I envision every possible way her body will surrender to me. Soon, very soon, I will know her body even more intimately. *Just as she will know mine...*

I stand close beside her as we leave her room and move through the hospital's corridors. Lila's steps are slow, weary from her recovery even though she's healed far faster than most humans. But each step she takes draws her deeper into my world, and I relish it. The anticipation that builds between us as questions and uncertainties fill her mind. The chaos begins to spiral within her, stirring my desire and accelerating my pace.

I place my hand on the small of her back, possessive and firm as I gently urge her to go a little faster. A silent reminder of who she now belongs to, of who she must now obey. I can feel the warmth of her body beneath her clothes. Her pulse quickens slightly under my touch, though whether it is from fear or something else, I can not tell and I don't feel the need to ask. *Not yet.*

The duality of her strength and fragility only makes me want her more. I want to see how far I can push her. *Will she survive? Could she really be the one?*

Leaning in slightly, I press my lips close to her ear and feel a shudder run through her body. She doesn't need words to understand what my touch conveys. This is no act of affection; it is a claim. I am marking my territory, claiming what is mine for all to see. No one else will ever have her the way I will. No one else will ever again touch her, break her, or make her kneel for their pleasure like I intend to do.

The air between us crackles with tension as we approach the exit. Her sense of freedom from the oppressiveness of the hospital is palpable. So tangible to her, and yet, it couldn't be further from the truth. She will never be free again, and I know she won't run. It was in our agreement, and she has nowhere else to go anyway. What I have offered is too much for her to pass up, and soon, I will show her the true meaning of captivity.The kind that doesn't come with chains, but with whispers in the shadows, with touches that linger far too long, with a hunger that will consume her soul. I will find her weaknesses, those loose pieces of string that will unravel her entirely… and I will be the one to put her back together.

As the hospital doors slide open, my grip on her shoulder tightens slightly. She flinches as if she'd forgotten I was there, but it brings a smirk to my lips as I guide her out into the night. The cool air hits us like a wave, but the heat between us burns strong, just beneath the surface. I smile, amused by the idea that she still has no idea that, once we leave this place, she will be walking into something much darker than she can fathom. *My world.*

CHAPTER SIX

LILA

Nyler already seems so possessive of me, and it's both frightening and exhilarating. I've never wanted someone so much in my life. The way he looks at me has me imagining things probably better left in the gutter, and his touch does something to me I can't explain. I've never liked being touched before, even though I crave true affection. But when he touches me, I feel myself turning into butter, like I'm ready to just give him everything, all that I am. I have to actively stop myself from melting into him, from looking too desperate…

As the hospital doors slide open his fingers grip my shoulder and I flinch, as though I'm expecting a beating the moment I'm back out in the world. I look around for a would-be assailant, but all I see, lit up by the street lights, are rows of cars spaced out in the parking lot.

Then, beneath one of the lights, I spot movement. There are men, dressed in black, standing by a black Chrysler with tinted black windows.

What did I expect from a mafia man?

One of the men quickly opens the door, allowing me to enter first. I slide into the seat and Nyler quickly climbs in beside me on the driver's side. His intense gaze meets mine and butterflies erupt all over again. We stare at each other for a moment as the car begins to move. Over and over again, I replay in my mind how his hand had felt, and wonder if any of it was real. *Do I want it to be real?*

"Lila?" Nyler's voice breaks through the silence and I realize my heart is pounding. "Are you alright?"

I simply nod, wondering what will be in store for me when we arrive at his place. And it seems I spent a while lost in thought, because I surface from my mind as I feel the car come to a stop.

My door opens before I can even reach for the handle and I step out of the car in front of Club Void. Nyler comes up behind me and places a possessive hand on the small of my back as we move toward the club. I can hear the thump of the music just beyond the doors, and the second they open for us music filters out much louder, the base matching the pounding of my heart. Nyler guides us into the loud and dark space, and colorful lights illuminate a sea of people who jump and dance to the rave-like music. We're almost to the center of the room when a man dressed in a bright yellow suit steps toward us.

"What's this, Nyarl–"

"You will not disrespect me in my domain, Hastur," Nyler quickly snaps. "Why are you here? You know what happens when we occupy the same space!"

It's the first time I've heard Nyler raise his voice. The atmosphere seems to change and the people around us become more chaotic, dancing erratically while some even break out into fist fights.

This seems to amuse the man called Hastur. His eyes fall upon me again and something dark shifts in them. "She's…"

"Mine," Nyler answers, quickly wrapping an arm around me, moving us away from the man.

"Not for long!" Hastur calls out after us with a wicked grin.

We move to the far end of the club where Nyler opens a door and guides me inside. He leads me halfway down a hall before we turn, stopping at an elevator door. My brows furrow as we step in, and more questions fill me.

"Promise me you'll stay far away from that man if you ever see him again." I can see the deep concern in his eyes, and it almost frightens me. *Is that guy more dangerous than Nyler?*

My eyebrows raise, but I nod. "I promise."

Nyler's gaze softens. "Good girl." The praise goes straight to the butterflies in my stomach, and then to my core which clenches, aching with need. It feels like my body is losing control.

"Lila?" Nyler says as he takes my hand and leads me into his home.

"Yes, Nyler?" I finally say, making sure to say his name since he's said mine so much.

His lips curve. "You will enjoy it here, I promise, but…I need to stake my claim on you, right now."

"What do you mean?"

"What do you think I mean, Lila?"

"S-sex?" I question, my fingers fidgeting against my stomach.

Nyler nods slowly and stalks towards me. "I'm afraid I can't wait any longer."

Before I can even say anything, Nyler bends and picks me up into his arms, carrying me bridal-style across the threshold of his room. A small gasp escapes my lips and it has him grinning, even as his eyes burn through me with desire.

I'm placed on the bed and Nyler lays over me. His hand slides up my dress, and a gasp leaves my lips as his fingers easily penetrate me again.

He leans into my ear and whispers, "I'm not human,

Lila. I wanted our first time to be while I was in human form, but I'm afraid I can't wait for that."

I feel my body shudder at his words and his touch as he strokes me deeply. I feel the same sensations as before. Multiple finger-like appendages that are far too malleable moving within me. I groan out loud, enjoying the pleasure. "So I wasn't imagining things?" I say breathlessly.

Nyler shakes his head. "No. You weren't. Do you think you can accept me as I am? In my true form?"

I pause momentarily, but nod, tamping my fear down.

His grin splits his face as his full set of teeth elongate into fangs. His entire form shifts, and in an instant, dark tentacles with a mind of their own fly up my dress. Others wrap around my arms and legs spreading them apart as wide as they will go and I'm wrapped up like bondage. *Similar to my dream...* In a flash, my dress is ripped off of me and I'm lifted into the air, suspended like a puppet on display. My heart beats wildly in both fear and excitement.

When I look at him, I don't even get to fully take in his changed form before I'm brought down on his girthy and unusual-looking cock. Even it has smaller tentacles... I let out a high-pitched gasp as I'm impaled onto it, feeling it slither inside of me, its pointed tip forcing its way into my cervix as deeply as it can possibly go. I cry out in pain, but it is quickly overshadowed by the deep pleasure I feel as every part of me is filled with him, just as every part of my skin is being caressed. My nipples pebble under the efforts of a few of the tentacles, while my anus is teased and eventually probed.

I'm dazed, riding high like I'm on a new kind of drug and I feel like I could break apart, shattering into a million pieces with every thrust. His voice calls to me, reaching into the depths where I usually hide. It reverberates in my mind even though his toothy grin doesn't move, and I know he's in my head.

"You are incredible, Lila. I've waited so long to find you."

I glance down at my stomach and can see a bulge protrude with each of his thrusts as he stretches me to my absolute limits. Again, each part of him seems to pulsate with life, and it is unlike anything I've ever felt before. I can feel the smaller tentacles writhing within me, teasing my walls as the smaller ones at the base of his cock tease my sensitive clit. I quickly come to terms with the fact that this is reality, not a dream, and I now belong to some kind of alien. I let go, and allow myself to revel in the pleasure of the pain.

. . .

Pain that reaches into every part of me as he becomes rougher. The tentacles wrapping around my legs feel like they could rip them from my hips, and I groan as I get closer to heaven. I've endured so much pain in my life, but nothing like this. This is the kind of pain I could get lost in.

I cry out as I'm brought to my climax, and feel Nyler's strange cock throb, swell, and release, filling me up with a deep guttural growl that sounds other-worldly. And I guess it is... He gently lowers me back to the bed, then collapses over me, panting as he returns to his human form.

The earth shakes beneath us and Nyler sets up abruptly before running across the room to his computer. With a wave of his hand, I'm cleaned up and dressed again, and so is he. His fingers fly across the keyboard.

I finally manage to climb out of the bed and join him. "What is it? What's wrong?"

"He's awake..."

"Who?" I breathe, feeling alarmed, still reeling from such intense pleasure.

"Cthulhu." He turns to me. "And I think I know why."

"Cth—" I pause, not even trying to attempt that name. "Why?"

"You survived." He stands suddenly and paces the floor before stopping and staring at me intently. "They know you exist now. More will come..."

To be continued in the full version...

Dedicated to all the freaks like me.

PROMISE OF A SNAKE GOD

STEFANIE DAWN

CHAPTER ONE

Every bump of the carriage over imperfections in the road was agony.

Not because of the physical discomfort, but because each bump served as a harsh reminder against my backside that I was closer to our final destination, where I would meet the man I was to marry. Despite the ending fairy tales promised me, I would not be marrying my true love. Nor marrying for love at all, in fact, but instead for money. As the youngest of the family and the only daughter unwed, I was perfect to be offered up to join two families who decided their individual fortunes simply would not do.

William Cushing. We managed one scheduled telephone conversation that lasted exactly five minutes and thirty-two seconds. I knew because I'd been counting until I could end the conversation with perhaps the most arrogant man I'd ever spoken to. Adding to my irritation was that the entire time he'd insisted on calling me Esther, and when I requested he called me Essie, the silence on the line had been dotted only with interference.

Sighing, I leaned my head against the side of the carriage as a wheel skipped over another rock in the underdeveloped road – a long, lonely stretch that crossed the majority of the sixty mile-plus journey between my husband-to-be and I.

Bump. Bump. Bump.

I almost settled into the seat again after a particularly rough lurch, when a squeal was torn from my throat after a violent jerk of the carriage. The horses who drew it gave equal cries of alarm as Mr. Archer the coachman shouted, "Whoa!"

We came to a complete stop and before my escort – Uncle Herbert – could argue, I had clicked open the small brass latch on the door and hopped out of the carriage, stumbling only slightly on the uneven road in my heeled boots. As I regained myself, our day-man Potter jumped from the carriage to gather up the luggage which had been tossed from the roof when the horses startled, and I lifted my dress to avoid brushing on the road as I rushed forward to see the commotion.

Thankful I had my back to the men who were escorting me, I barely contained my delight at the friend who took up residence in a sunny spot in the middle of the road. The rattlesnake shook its tail menacingly where it sat, coiled as it hissed, and its tongue darted out toward the horses as they nervously moved away from the creature.

"I'll take care of it," Archer said as he patted one of the horses roughly on the flank before he reached up to pull his shotgun from his seat upon the carriage. "Stand clear."

"Wait!" The uncomfortable pause that followed my outcry was filled only with the continued rattle of the snake who wished to warn us off. Archer's eyes slid to where I stood. I dropped my dress and ignored how it dragged in the loose dust of the road as I raised my hands defensively. "It's frightened, can't you see?"

Archer glanced at the horses as they hoofed nervously at the dirt, the whites of their eyes gleaming. "O' course they are, Miss."

"Not them – the *snake*."

Archer's eyes widened a fraction more for a moment, before they narrowed at me. "The snake?"

"Yes," I said, and lifted my dress again as I stepped toward the reptile in the road. I swung my foot at it, hoping if it did strike out the leather of my boots would be enough to protect my ankles. "Shoo please," I said, and when the snake didn't move and only increased the threatening rattle of its tail, I repeated the motion. "Shoo. Out of the way."

I could feel Archer, Potter and Uncle Herbert's

stares at my back, and the judgment would surely be in their gaze at the ridiculous nature of my actions.

"Please, Mr. Snake," I whispered at him as I felt the heat rise in my cheeks. *"You're making me look bad."*

By now three pairs of eyes were boring holes into the back of my dress, and self-consciously I tucked a dark curl behind my ear as I stared the snake down. It was no longer rattling, but instead eyeing me warily.

I was either about to get bitten, or ignored again.

What I didn't expect was for the snake to unfurl and slither quietly off the road before it disappeared into the dense undergrowth of the forest.

"Well, I'll be..." Archer whispered, no doubt not intended for me to hear. The heated flush of my cheeks increased. Would news of this get to William, and what would he think of me if it did? Would he call the entire wedding off, not wanting to be married to someone who was mad enough to talk to a snake?

Did I even care?

Of course I did. This was beyond me and my feelings on the matter. I had the honor of my family on my shoulders, along with the future of two large oil companies coming together.

All riding on the simple act of me accepting a ring onto my finger.

Although I couldn't help the flare of hope in my chest at the mere *idea* of cancelation.

After a beat, I straightened and brushed an imaginary speck of dirt from my sleeve. Before I turned to face my escorts, my lips almost lifted into a smile as I resisted the temptation to wave merrily in the direction the snake had gone. If they thought me mad, the improper thing to do would be to play into it.

Pressing my lips together and gathering as much control as I could, I lifted my dress from the ground again and turned toward the carriage. "Shall we?" I said.

Archer shook his head as if to shake himself from a stupor, while Potter set to work checking the horses were firmly strapped in place. Uncle Herbert simply raised a brow at me over his glasses, before he too shook his head and returned to the carriage.

Pausing briefly before I stepped back inside, I turned and faced the forest, and offered a small curtsey toward the dark shadows.

Thank you for moving, Mr. Snake.

CHAPTER TWO

We stopped for the night at a small inn.

The horses were set up in the stable, and the freckled innkeeper with generous cleavage on display in a way that both startled me and made me smile – and wished I had the courage to ask Father for a dress like that – showed me to my room out the back. Uncle tried insisting on a room upstairs, but no amount of huffing and tapping his foot impatiently changed the fact there were simply no available rooms. Meredith didn't give a *good goddamn,* as I'd heard her mumble, *who* my Uncle was, she wasn't going to displace paying customers just because someone demanded something other than the smaller rooms out back.

Meredith returned my smile as she held the door open to my simple but comfortable room. "Dinner is served from six, dear. No rush. I'll make sure to save you some soup."

"Thank you, madam." I curtsied.

"Surely I should be the one doin' that," Meredith said with a chuckle before she copied my motion with much less grace, but more enthusiasm. I giggled quietly as she closed the door behind her and turned to face my empty room. Only when given the chance to be in silence did the ache in my legs and backside become prominent. The carriage was luxurious, but still not comfortable for an entire day's journey, and we had another full day of traveling ahead.

Sighing, I dropped myself onto the bed, and the old wood creaked as it shifted slightly on the floor. I would ask for hot water to run a bath later, but right now I simply wished I was home, and I flopped back to lie on the lumpy mattress and stared up at the ceiling.

I blinked.

The ceiling stared back.

Narrowing my eyes, I focused on the shadows created by the panels, and saw the yellow eyes of a small snake looking down at me.

"Oh, hello." I released a heavy breath before it shifted into a chuckle. "You must think me terribly dramatic, to keep sighing like this." Another sigh, then another laugh. Once I'd brought it to my attention, it was impossible not to focus on how often I did it. "I have nothing to complain about, really. A life of boredom is better than no life at all." The snake, of course, didn't answer, and simply continued to stare at me. "I met one of your friends earlier, he startled our horses something fierce. Thankfully I was able to shoo him away without any harm." I raised a hand to my mouth as I yawned. "Who would've thought sitting in a carriage all day would be so tiring?"

I had an hour before dinner was being served. Perhaps I deserved a small nap.

No sooner did I have the thought than I dropped off to sleep.

It was far darker than I would've expected for this time of day, unless I had slept through dinner and into the night? Blinking as though that would clear the darkness, I sat up on the edge of the bed and smoothed the sheets out behind me where I'd lay.

My hand stilled as the rattle of a rattlesnake's tail whispered at me through the darkness.

Maybe Uncle had been right to want an upstairs room. Here I was at the mercy of anything that could crawl or slither through the gap under the door.

Slowly, I lifted my feet from the ground and glanced around in the darkness, trying to force myself to remember if I'd seen a lamp somewhere nearby.

What little light there was in the room was obscured

further as a shadow moved in front of me. A man's silhouette, so dark the shadows were forced away and replaced by his presence as he leaned over me. When he breathed out, a rush of cold air accompanied a dangerous hiss, and as I opened my mouth to scream, his hand clasped over my face.

I'm asleep, and this is a nightmare.

Air coming in rapid gasps through my nose, I forced myself to calm.

Just a dream.

I was forced to lay back on the bed as his form moved over me, and the rattle behind him increased in intensity as he hummed. The press of his chest over my torso was heavy, and I barely had time to register that his chest was bare. A sharp intake of air moved through my nose as I gasped.

Was he naked?

I had dreams of this nature before, though my cheeks heated to admit it even to myself. But never a shadow of a man that leaned over me in the darkness. More a faceless being, dressed as a prince who kneeled in front of me and confessed his undying love. Sometimes he was a pirate like in the stories from my childhood, and he'd whisk me away to his ship, where he'd lay me down and kiss me passionately…

My eyes widened as the man above me flicked his tongue out.

Forked, thin, and long, like that of a snake.

Hands clenching the sheets on either side of my body, I debated if I should attack, or simply let the dream play out. Dangerous and forbidden thoughts played through my mind, and I felt a warmth between my legs as his torso pressed against me.

My brows drew together, his torso seemed much too long…

"You are ssstunning…" he hissed the words out on another breath, and I gasped again.

This is such a strange dream.

Forcing myself to look away from his naked chest and at his face, he stared down at me with his bright eyes.

Yellow eyes, with slits for pupils.

"You do not belong here," he whispered to me in that dark voice that had me trembling under his hold. My eyes widened as he spoke. His hand was still firmly pressed over my mouth, and when I tried to speak, he removed it. He did so slowly, one finger at a time as though after each inch he was waiting for me to scream. When I didn't, he traced his fingers down the side of my cheek and over my neck. With a shudder, I arched into his touch, and he brushed his palm ever so gently over my breast before he pulled his hand away.

"Who are you?" I asked, whispering as he had.

"You saved one of my children instead of allowing it to be killed." Before I could ask anything further, he hissed again, his tongue once more flicked out of his mouth and tasted the air between us. "Do you want to come away with me?"

"Where?" My chest rose and fell rapidly against his, breathless with anticipation. Perhaps this dream was a fairytale after all, though darker than I usually imagined. I could barely think straight. My pull to this man on top of me was magnetic.

I *did* want to go away with him, wherever he wanted to go, I didn't care.

Take me away...

The words were on the edge of my lips.

"Live with me... let me love you. Life is wild, but I promise you'll be happy."

I swallowed heavily. "Wild?"

He chuckled, a sound edged with a hiss and over-ridden only by the enticing rattle that came from behind him again. "What is your name?"

"Esther." I shook my head slightly. "Essie. Call me Essie."

"Essssie... do you believe in fate?"

"Should I?" I almost jerked on the mattress as I reminded myself to breathe.

"Are you happy, Essssie? Or shall I come for you tonight and take you away with me?"

"Is this a dream?"

He shushed me with a gentle hiss. "Let me take care of you."

I trembled as he lowered himself, until his face was

level with the gentle flare of my hips, and hastily I grabbed the edge of my dress and held it in place. He hissed again, and I stilled as his hands covered mine before he guided the fabric up and over my knees, then my thighs, until finally he bundled it over my lower stomach. I squealed as he tugged my undergarments down and out of the way. The warmth between my legs was unbearable, and I was torn between desire to rub my thighs together, or to part my legs for him. I released a small squeak at the idea of exposing myself to this man, even in a dream, and was snapped from my thoughts as his hands found my thighs and encouraged me to spread my legs.

He leaned in to inhale deeply, and his forked tongue darted out. I jerked again as it flicked over my skin. Cautiously, he used his fingers to part the lips of my cunt, and stared intently as though I were a prize to be claimed. As I opened my mouth to object to the obscene gesture, his tongue flicked out again, and licked between the lips of my cunt.

My entire body jerked and my fingers grabbed handfuls of the bed sheets and I glanced down with wide eyes to find him smiling up at me.

"Ssspread your legssss wider…"

I complied, even as I trembled, and his hands guided me with a firm grip on my thighs. When I was spread for him, he dove down and began lapping at my cunt as though it was the most precious ambrosia. Every time his tongue would flick over me, my hips would jerk against him.

"What are you doing?" I gasped as I writhed.

"Licking your clit…"

After minutes of the pleasurable torment, I found myself pushing at his shoulders and head, and tried to get him to stop. The feeling was too intense, and every time he licked it was like a shock through my body, and I feared if he kept going I would explode.

But he wouldn't stop.

I cried out when he angled his head so he could shove his tongue inside me. It was thin, but still enough for my body to rebel against. I'd never so much as inserted a finger into myself, though much to my shame the thought crossed my mind once or twice.

His tongue wiggled inside me, and I felt moisture from my arousal sticky on my thighs. I sighed with relief as he withdrew his tongue, and the torture of the impending sensation eased.

I tried to clench my legs closed as he started licking my clit again.

"It's too much," I cried out, and pushed at his head as though I had any chance of moving him. He was a solid force against me, and his grip on my thighs grew stronger as he looked up at me over my body as he feasted on my cunt. He pulled away only long enough to hiss at me as I struggled. "It's too much. Something's happening – please stop!"

His pupils dilated.

My back arched, and my head pressed back against the bed as the explosion happened, and his hand slapped over my mouth as I screamed through a burst of pleasure so intense it bordered on pain. When I thought it couldn't possibly go on, it came again in waves, and crashed over my body until I convulsed.

When he finally moved his mouth and tongue away from my cunt, I slumped, panting heavily. Slowly, he rose and came back over me, and pressed his body against me as I trembled. I blinked up at him as he hovered over me, and he answered my unasked question. "I made you come."

"Who are you?" I panted out.

But he only hissed his satisfaction. "You tassste perfect..."

A sharp knock on the door broke the trance, and I sat bolt upright.

The shadows cleared, the man was gone, and I was alone again in my room.

"Dinner, Esther," my Uncle called through the closed door.

"Oh, uh, coming!" I called back, desperately smoothing out the rumpled state of my dress as I stood. I blinked a few times and rubbed my eyes. The light outside from the setting sun was rapidly dwindling.

What a strange dream.

I wished it hadn't ended so soon.

CHAPTER THREE

Sleep didn't come easy, and I tossed and turned under the scratchy bedsheet in my nightgown. Finally, I huffed, flopped heavily onto my back, and stared at the ceiling. The snake from earlier was gone – assuming it had been there at all and wasn't simply another waking dream. A dream I couldn't seem to will myself to accept wasn't real.

I'd figured out who the mystery man was, or so I thought, but it seemed so bizarre I hadn't yet allowed myself a moment to be still and let the name drift into my mind.

Yig.

It was the only explanation. I encountered a snake on my journey, and the experience had reminded me of the legends, and he'd simply floated into my mind fully formed as a dream. I'd never had course to imagine him before, but the idea he was a dark and foreboding man who came to visit me in my bed certainly fit the image of a serpent god that could lure me into forbidden temptation and pleasure.

When the door of my room opened, I stilled, hoping whoever it was wouldn't be able to see the whites of my eyes reflected off what meager light crept in from the hall.

But it was him.

The room grew cold, and I clutched the blanket and pulled it up under my chin as a child would, as though that would save me from whatever this apparition was.

The knowledge this wasn't a dream hit me with such clarity I dared not question it.

His body filled the doorframe, and shoulders scraped past the wood as he entered my room. Yig didn't walk, he *slithered* through the doorway. For the extended torso I thought I had imagined earlier was revealed now to be where his chest simply flowed gracefully into a large tail.

Half man, half snake.

I couldn't find the breath nor the will to utter a sound, and my eyes grew wider when Yig came up to the side of my bed, yet the shadowy shape of the length of his tail still curled across the floor and out the open door.

He was *magnificent.*

"You," I whispered.

He held a hand out to me. "Come with me."

It wasn't a demand, simply more softly spoken words, as if I had a chance of resisting the lure I felt to him. The memory of his tongue on my cunt had my lip trembling, and I lowered the sheet down my body. I shuddered as the cool air hit my arms as I exposed myself to him. Though I wasn't naked, the gesture wasn't lost on Yig. His tongue darted out of his mouth again, and explored the space between us as though he could taste me on the air.

I was offering myself to him.

"What's happening?" He would know, surely. He would be able to explain this pull between us, and why the tremble of my body wasn't of fear, but anticipation.

"You're mine Essssie, if you wish to be…"

"Where will you take me?"

"To my home." He sounded almost thoughtful, and I thought I caught a glimpse of a fang reflected in the dull light as he smiled. "Where I will pleasure you, and we will live together, forever…"

"But…my family?"

With speed that had me gasping, he was on top of me, and the press of his weight made the bed creak in protest as he lay across me. Yig braced his arms on either side of my head, and paused only to take a hungry intake of breath as his tongue darted out again. His entire body trembled as he groaned. "I do not wish to force you, Essssie…but I fear I cannot leave without you."

Wild, but happy.

I swallowed. *Why am I even considering this?*

"And…" I swallowed again, unable now to stop the tremble of my body under his. "If I'm not happy?"

"Then I will let you go." Again, he spoke gently, but his eyes flashed with dangerous promise. "But you must let me bring you pleasure first, before you say you wish to leave."

The silence stretched out between us while Yig waited for my answer.

What do I have to lose?

Your life, a voice in my head answered.

He won't hurt me.

I don't know how I knew, I simply knew.

This is your chance at the adventure you dreamed of.

This is a risk, the voice of reason answered.

But every time I breathed in, my breasts would brush against his chest. The rattle started again, and I realized it came from *his* tail. I took a deep breath with the intention of grounding myself in reality. Instead my lungs filled with the scent of him, and it was too much. I coughed, and convulsed slightly under where his body pressed against mine. Yig hissed gently, and his tongue swiped out to lick up the length of my neck. He smelled of earth and musk, of the forest and soil, and of something I couldn't quite place but I imagined could only be the scent of arousal.

And *sex*.

I was drugged by the scent of him, and his face came into sharper focus as my pupils dilated. Yig was handsome, as much as he could be. A sharp jawline and cheekbones, but a barely-there nose that wasn't much more than two slits for nostrils on a small bump. His eyes were large and yellow, and his pupils widened as he watched me take him in.

I found myself wanting to touch him, and to find out what he looked like with the sunlight spread across his monstrous body. I'd wager he'd be magnificent, a dappled mixture of browns and black, smooth scales that begged to be touched.

"Yes," I whispered, and Yig hummed his approval, before he wrapped his arms around me, tucked me against his body, and fled from the room.

The inn disappeared from my sight, swallowed up by the darkness faster than if I'd traveled by carriage and the horses were at full gallop. The night air rushed through my hair, and I tucked my head against Yig's chest, unable to do much else. His arms tightened around me where he held my body against his, and I dared a glance up at his face as he moved. The few moments I had of taking in his handsome features were cut short when he crossed the threshold into the forest, and what little light the moon offered was gone.

An hour, perhaps longer, we moved, and whenever I had a moment of unease, I would press my cheek against his chest and inhale deeply. That scent was enough to calm me, to intoxicate me in ways I'd never considered before. That warmth returned between my legs, and I resisted the urge to slide a hand between them. I settled for rubbing my thighs together, but instead of relieving the tension and discomfort, it only increased it.

Yig hissed above me, and I looked up to find his yellow eyes on me.

"Sssoon," he whispered, and I nodded, though I wasn't sure what he meant.

The forest closed in around us, and the density blocked out almost all available light. I tucked in against Yig, afraid I was going to get snagged or hit against a tree. But he moved through the forest as though he were part of it, twigs and undergrowth breaking under his tail as he slid deeper into the darkness.

When he stopped, he lowered me to the ground, I stood still, unable to see, and rubbed my chilled arms as he moved about. The first crackles of a fire started, and soon he had stoked it into a warm embrace that filled the area.

We were in a cave of some sort, created by rock

formations that offered protection from the weather and had only one entrance and exit.

An exit that was currently filled by the giant snake god that was Yig.

He towered above me, and as the area was warmed he approached me, and slowly lowered on his tail until his face was but a foot above mine. I tilted my chin up to look into his eyes.

"Is this home?"

"If you like it," he said. Even when he wasn't whispering, his voice was quiet and dark, and I felt he could command the attention on anyone he wished without ever having to raise it louder.

His hand came up to brush my arm, and on instinct I flinched from the touch. Immediately he pulled his hand away from me, and I chuckled nervously. "Sorry," I said, and looked at the ground.

Yig tilted my chin until I was looking into his eyes, and without removing his hold from my face he touched my arm again, and brushed his palm up until his fingers met the top of my nightgown.

When he pulled it down over my shoulder, I gasped. "What are you doing?"

Yig tilted his head. "I'm going to pleassssure you, Essssie."

"I...I..." My thighs pressed together as I squirmed on the spot, and trembled as Yig released my chin so he could slide the fabric off my shoulders. I clung to my dress before it could drop away from my body, and Yig hissed angrily. I screamed as he grabbed the front of the fabric and tore it with his claws, before he yanked the now shredded clothing from my body.

I was naked and exposed to him, and when I backed away, trying in vain to cover myself with my hands, Yig followed until my back hit the cave wall.

"Do not run from me, Essssie…" he whispered, and for the first time there was menace in his words. "You promised I could pleasure you, and make you happy."

"I didn't… I've never –"

"Sssshh…" Yig reached down, cupped his hands under my backside, and lifted me, forcing my legs to spread to make room for the girth of his body and he pressed forward. I was trapped between the rocks and the hard lines of his chest. "I will take care of you."

I nodded, and despite the warmth of the fire I was unable to keep from trembling. When there was an insistent pressing under my breasts, and I looked down to see the scales on Yig's stomach had parted.

"Yig!" I cried out, raising my hands to cover my mouth as my jaw dropped. "There are *two of them.*"

CHAPTER FOUR

Yig looked down when I continued to stare, as his two hard members bobbed just underneath my exposed breasts. They were easily each as thick and long as my forearm, and ended in a series of spurs, the heads an angry pink that slowly faded into the deep brown of the rest of his scales.

"Yesss. Humans do not have two."

It wasn't a question, but I responded anyway. "No!" I was aghast at the thought, and pressed my back against the wall as though that would help me get further away. All the ideas of pleasure were pushed to the side, though I still felt my cunt getting wet, and I tensed as a drop of creamy fluid dripped from the head of one of his members.

Tentatively and unable to stop myself, I reached forward and touched one of the spurs. It was fleshy and soft, and I breathed a sigh of relief; I wasn't about to get torn apart.

But the *size...*

Not to mention…

"Yig," I started, my voice trembling. "You know humans only have one…" I struggled to find the word, *"entrance,* right?"

I yelped as Yig's hand gripped my backside where he held me, and lifted me up slightly so his members rubbed between my thighs. I groaned, and was unable to stop myself from grinding my hips obscenely against him. His tail circled up around me, and wrapped around my torso, and held me steady as my hips moved desperately.

Apparently, my body was no longer within my control.

Being held up by his tail left Yig's hands free to explore.

He brushed his fingers between my legs, and finding the entrance to my cunt he pushed a thick finger inside. I squealed, and tried to kick my legs out. "Careful!" I cried out as I gripped his shoulders. "I've never done this before."

"It's only my finger… and you need to be ssstretched if you're to take my cocksss."

I squeezed my eyes shut and tried to ignore he'd used the plural as he worked his finger in and out of my cunt. I trembled around the intrusion, and slowly the sensation eased from sharp pain into pleasure.

"That'sss it…" he encouraged me, and licked up my neck again.

The rattle sounded again, and I looked down to see the end of his tail moving down my stomach and between my legs. His entire lower body shifted, and the smooth slide of his scales rubbed against my skin and he wound himself around me, and eased his tail lower between my legs.

As he removed his finger, the tip of his tail pushed against my cunt and sought entrance. I dropped my hands from his shoulders and gripped where his tail coiled around my torso, my nails digging into his skin.

"Too much…" I grit my teeth as his tail pushed inside. I widened my legs to accompany the stretch, and the texture of his rattle made each press further inside me a bump to mark another inch.

Bump. Bump. Bump.

"Stop. *Please.*" Mercifully Yig stilled as I squirmed where I was impaled on him, unable to get away from the intrusion that stretched me open.

"Relax, Essssie," he hissed out, and slowly he started to fuck me with his tail, a gentle rubbing motion that shifted him in and out only slightly. "You need to be ssstretched out."

I whimpered as the pain gave way to discomfort, and then to pleasure. The ridges of his tail rubbed against a sensitive spot inside me, and I bit my lip as I tried to tilt my hips to get *more* of that sensation. Yig chuckled, and he held my hips still until I huffed with frustration. His tongue came out again and licked the sweat that beaded on my neck and forehead.

I sighed into his touch, and relaxed against the stretch.

Yig started exploring with his fingers again, and I was yanked unceremoniously from my pleasured stupor when his finger pressed against my asshole.

He hummed. "You *do* have two holes…"

I squirmed against him again, but this only helped him to rub those delicious ridges of his tail inside me again, and I moaned at the sensation. "That's – that's not an entrance."

"No?" He pushed his finger inside me, and my muscles clenched against the intrusion as I cried out again. He let the tip of his finger still there inside me before he hummed again. "Ssseems to me it feels good for you, Essssie…your cunt is convulsing around my tail."

"I don't…you shouldn't!" But my eyes rolled back into my head as he twisted his tail inside me and hit that delectable spot again, and the burst of pleasure was only increased by the tight invasion of my asshole.

He chuckled and removed his finger, and I slumped as his tail slid out of my cunt, leaving me limp, empty, and aching.

"You're going to take my cocks now…"

My senses went into overdrive at his words, and the warmth from the fire burning behind Yig felt abruptly stronger against my legs where they were wrapped around his body. Yig's skin was cool to the touch, and my fingers danced over the smooth scales of his tail where it wrapped around my torso. I sighed as he adjusted me, and his tail brushed the underside of my breasts.

"Do you want me to fuck you?"

I gasped and looked into his eyes, heavy with desire, his pupils large as he stared at where our bodies met and his members pressed against the apex of my thighs. I *did* want him, and my body heated with desire that made me shudder as I clenched around nothing, wishing I again had the pleasure of his tail inside me.

Eyeing the spurs of his cock, I bit my lip.

"It'll feel good, right?" I asked, and my teeth grazed my bottom lip.

"I wish to give you nothing but pleasssure."

No dream could compare to this.

The reality of my responsibilities to my family stabbed in the back of my consciousness, trying to force themselves to the forefront of my mind against the heavy heat of pleasure that surrounded my body.

Yet, I shifted my hips, and invited this monster of a man, of a God, to take my virginity.

Yig hissed again, and the sound drew out as he held

me still with his tail, and used his hand to guide the head of his top member against my cunt. I tensed, and braced myself for pain I knew would come, but it would lead to pleasure.

"Relax, Essssie… I've got you."

"Just one, okay?" I whispered.

His lip lifted into a smirk. "For now…"

As I exhaled, he pushed his hips forward, and the head of his member sank inside me. A sharp pain had me trying to close my legs around his body, an impossible feat. But Yig did not stop and continued to press forward until the entire length of him disappeared inside me, one agonizing inch at a time. I jerked and trembled, and my hands grasped at his tail as I whimpered and moaned around the sensation. He was everywhere now, and everything, filling me up completely and impossibly, his tail around my body, and my legs around his. When he pulled back, I cried out again, and my cunt clenched, wishing to keep him inside despite the pain. The soft spurs molded inside me, and seemed to find every nerve and enhance every sensation.

Yig thrust forward, and sank fully inside me with a harsh motion.

"Go slow!" I squealed, and gripped his tail harder.

"I can't…" His words ended on another long hiss, and he pulled back again, only to thrust into me harder. My legs were being forced wider apart by the hardness of his body where his torso became his tail, and I was at the mercy of him as he fucked me against the rocks. I tried unsuccessfully to mask my moans, certain the sound would travel through the forest, and someone would be able to hear me. But I couldn't hide the sounds of pleasure for long. My back arched, and I let go of his tail to brace my palms against the rocky wall behind me, thankful for the cushioning of his hold on me. Yig used me, holding me body where he needed me to fuck in hard and deep, and stretched me beyond what I thought possible.

His thrusts became sporadic, and when he started grabbing at his second member I looked down in alarm. "What are you doing?"

Yig tried to guide his second member to my backside, and I cried out in surprise at the pressure against my hole before his member simply slipped between my cheeks. He tried again to the same result, and hissed angrily when he couldn't penetrate me.

Before I could speak, his tail was unraveling from me, the drag of his cool skin against mine adding another sensation while he continued to stretch me. When he pulled out of me, I couldn't stop the wail of "*No...*" that escaped my lips. I wasn't ready to be done yet, I'd only just begun to embrace the stretch of him and feel everywhere he hit inside.

Yig chuckled and shushed me gently. "Ssshhh... I'm only repositioning you."

He maneuvered himself around me until the bulk of

his tail was raised and I could lay back on it. Again, I was supported entirely by him, and with the coolness of his scales against my back, my legs flopped open in invitation as he slithered over me.

Cushioning me from the ground with his tail, he penetrated my cunt again with the top of his two members and gave a few hard thrusts until I was crying out and another peak of pleasure rose inside me.

I was going to *come.*

He pulled almost all the way out and reached between us to line his second member up with my asshole.

"Yig..." I tensed, and he simply hummed as he rubbed his member between my cheeks.

"This angle is better, I can fuck both your holes at the same time."

My jaw dropped, but I uttered no protest as he used the juices from my cunt to cover his lower member and pressed it against my rear entrance.

"It won't fit," I protested as he pushed.

"It'll fit." It was a promise, and my body was losing the fight to keep him out.

My voice was edged with a whimper. "It'll hurt."

Yig rubbed his thumb in circles over my clit, and I bucked my hips against his touch. His chuckle was dark, and as he continued rubbing the warmth flushed between my legs, wetness dripping down my thighs and over his tail where I lay. "I'll make you come so hard you'll forget any pain."

"I… I…" I was already losing the will to question him, and my eyes rolled back as he continued rubbing that spot. When I closed my eyes, I felt him leaning against me with the heads of both his members poised at my holes.

"Say pleassse…" he whispered, and my eyes snapped open to see the dark smirk on his face.

"*Please,*" I begged. The teasing circles of his thumb were driving me crazy, and I needed release. I needed to be filled, to be completely overcome and undone by him.

When his member penetrated my asshole with a sharp stab, I screamed, and when I tried to get away the end of his tail came over my stomach and held me down.

"Stay ssstill…" Yig grunted, and his hands stopped their delicious ministrations to grab my thighs and push my legs back. "Let me take you, Essssie…"

Tears slid down the side of my face as he pushed further forward, and my asshole and cunt opened up to him, completely at the mercy of his forceful push. His members seemed to harden further, and when with another harsh thrust his hips met my body, I screamed.

"There…" he began thrusting immediately. The pain in my backside clashed with the pleasure in my cunt, and I sobbed even as I moaned. "You're taking both my cocks so well, Essssie."

His thumb returned to rub infuriating circles on my clit, and coupled with his thrusts and the rub of his spurs inside me, my eyes rolled back in my head as I fell completely under his spell. There was no dream or nightmare that could compare to the exquisite pleasure that encompassed me now. There was nothing left of me, but to be *his.* If I were to spend my days impaled on his members, on the edge of absolute pleasure, then there'd be no greater life.

"Come for me," he demanded, and pressed harder with his thumb. "*Come for me.*"

I screamed again as I fell over the edge of the peak, and Yig's hands gripped my thighs as he fucked into me harder, both his members moving in and out in tandem. My screams and cries molded and faded, and when Yig groaned and I felt a rush of hot liquid inside me, my screams rose again when he started to swell.

"It hurts," I panted as my hands scrambled for purchase, and I settled on gripping his tail where it wrapped around my body. My holes were being thoroughly used by him, and I looked down in alarm as he pushed hard into me, and the sensation of swelling increased. "*What's happening?*"

"My knots," he answered as if it were obvious. He threw his head back and squeezed his eyes shut. "To keep my seed inside you."

Before I could question, I came again, a rush of pleasure I wasn't prepared for so soon, and Yig hissed happily as he pushed in that little bit further, and the knot that swelled at the base of his member sank into my cunt. I tried to spread my legs to ease the pressure to no avail, and was caught between pleasure and pain as Yig's member pulsed inside me. I could feel his knot pressing insistently against my asshole, but there was no way it would fit, and I was silently thankful he wasn't forcing it.

Pulse after pulse of liquid splashed inside me, and my eyes widened as I watched my stomach bloat with the volume of his seed. Each pulse made his spurs rub inside me, and when I started lolling my head from side to side, Yig hissed as he started rubbing my clit with his thumb again. "Come."

"Again? I can't."

"Come, or I'll force my knot into your second hole..."

The words shouldn't have turned me on, but the idea of being even *more* stretched by him had me coming again, and the rush of my juices squeezed around his knot.

I slumped, completely void of any energy, and after moments of silence only broken by Yig's satisfied hissing, he started to pull back. I whimpered as his members pulled from my holes, and the rush of his come spilled over my thighs and his tail. I squeezed my eyes shut, embarrassed, and tried to cover myself with my hands. Yig hissed angrily, and with his tail still around my torso tilted me upward so he could lick the juices from my thighs. The lash of his hot tongue against my skin was exquisite.

Yig lowered me as he coiled himself, lay me down in the comfort of his tail next to the fire, and I sighed heavily. My cunt and asshole pulsed. I felt used and emptied, but satisfied in a way I never imagined possible.

"I'm so tired Yig…" I whispered as I lifted my hand to cover my yawn.

"Sleep, Essssie. Tomorrow I'll force both my members into your tight cunt."

I clenched at his words, imagining the pleasure as I smiled and closed my eyes. "Okay…"

"Almost there Essssie." Yig's fingers flexed on my hips as I straddled him. My face was screwed up as I panted rapidly, and tried to force my body to relax. I glanced down, both of his members were pressed together, and were sunk halfway inside my cunt.

We'd spent three days in Yig's home, eating, sleeping, and fucking, and not much else. While I'd slept the first night, Yig had returned to the Inn and grabbed a handful of my clothes. When I explained to him what he'd returned with were both nightgowns and held up the thin white garment to show him, he'd simply hissed at me.

"I want you naked anyway."

As promised, the second day with him he'd tried – unsuccessfully – to force both his members into my cunt. He'd hissed out in frustration when it wouldn't work, before he soothed me and licked my neck and face as I apologized profusely.

"I'll just have to stretch you out more..."

Halfway inside me now, and it was the furthest I'd taken them. The constant tremble of my legs turned into a jerk with each inch he sank further inside, and any discomfort was forgotten as I let him guide my movements, and pleasure overwhelmed my senses.

"I'm going to... I'm sorry, I can't stop... I'm going to..."

"Yesss..." Yig groaned as I came around him again, and held me still as I convulsed on top of him. He used the moments after my orgasm to slide me further down onto his members, and I cried out as he started using me. He gripped my hips and lifted my body up and down, so he was thrusting in and out of me, mercifully only a few inches at a time.

Just when I thought he had taken me to the absolute peaks of pleasure, he found another way to take me further.

"Yig!" I screamed as his blunt claws dug into my thighs and he released an animalistic roar that set me on edge. "What's wrong?"

Yig's breathing was heavy, and his chest rose and fell rapidly as he stared down at where dots of blood appeared on my thighs. "Did I harm you?"

"I'm okay. What's wrong? What happened?"

"Someone'sss hurting my children."

"Who?"

He lifted me from him, and I whimpered as his members pulled out of my cunt. He slithered to his full height and placed me on my feet. As he tucked his members inside him, I stumbled as my legs shook from the aftershocks of multiple orgasms.

"Stay here," he demanded.

But I grabbed his arm as he turned to leave. "I want to go with you."

His pupils narrowed as he watched me, and after a tense moment he nodded curtly. In a rush I pulled a nightdress over my head, before I climbed into his waiting arms. The moment my feet left the ground, Yig sped off, and I tucked my face against his chest against the rush of warm air as he moved through the forest.

When he stopped, Yig lowered me to my feet as he stared ahead. I couldn't see anything but trees, but before I could open my mouth to question, I heard it. The unmistakable sound of vegetation being chopped away, as a group of people marched through the forest.

"Are they here for me?" I whispered and clung to Yig's arm. The reality I left behind had been pushed further into the back of my mind the more time I spent with Yig, and I didn't want to go back.

His tongue darted out. "Yesss…"

He slid between the trees, and I followed carefully behind him.

Peeking between two large branches, I saw William and a group of men slicing their way through the plants with machetes. When William stopped, his hand darted down between the shrubbery, and as he straightened, he held a small snake aloft.

My eyes widened.

With a sneer, William looked into the forest and held the snake out, and I covered my mouth to hide my scream as he sliced its head off.

The men waited, and when the forest answered only with silence, the dead snake was dropped and forgotten, and they surged forward.

"Are you certain of what you were told?" William barked to the man next to him.

"Absolutely, Sir. The peasant at the inn was insistent." He raised the pitch of his voice as he mimicked, "*It was Yig 'oo took her, I swear it, sir, swear it on me life.*" The man offered a sideways glance at William. "And you believe him? You believe the tales?"

"Yes," William said simply, and offered no further explanation. My brows furrowed. The legends were certainly prevalent, but I would've never expected a nobleman such as William to succumb to them.

Had he encountered Yig before?

When William stopped again and reached down to grab another small snake, I ducked under Yig's arm and rushed forward. "Stop!"

William's eyes widened before they narrowed, and

his gaze traveled down my body, taking in my torn and dirty nightgown, messy hair, and bare feet.

"Esther, thank the Lord you're safe." He tossed the snake to the side and ignored the alarmed cry of two men as they moved out of the way of the hissing reptile. "Come with me."

"No."

"No?" His perfect brow arched. "Esther, we are to be wed."

"I don't want to go with you."

He lurched forward and grabbed my wrist, and when I wouldn't move he tugged me forward. I fell to my knees and hissed through my teeth as my arms were scratched by the undergrowth. William tugged me to my feet, and turned with his machete at the ready as there was a roar behind me.

Yig's appearance from the shadows was accompanied by the sounds of half the men dropping their weapons and the crunch of plants as they fled.

William scowled. "She belongs with me, monster."

"Ssshe is mine."

I tried to yank my hand from William's grip. "William, let me go. I don't want to go with you."

"Haven't you heard the legends, Esther?"

My brows furrowed. *Of course I had. I knew the stories.*

William continued, whispering harshly against my ear. "He takes a bride every few decades to birth his many children. He keeps her until she dies. Then he finds another."

Yig's eyes darted to mine, and my cunt pulsed. I couldn't help the smile that came. "Yig loves me."

"Let her go, human."

William's lips curved into an unsettling smile, but he ignored me as I continued to fight against his hold. "Come and get her, monster."

I stilled, and my wrist throbbed as William's grip increased as a wave of sound overtook the serenity of the forest around us. What remained of William's men shared equal looks of trepidation, and turned to head back the way they'd come as quickly as they could without outright sprinting. William's gaze slid to me as the hissing increased, and we glanced down to find the forest floor alive with snakes. Writhing and sliding over each other, building until they were at our calves.

I shrieked as William grabbed me, spun me around, and held my back against his chest. His blade came to my throat, and I tilted my head back to avoid the sharp edge of the machete.

"Call them off," he said to Yig, and I whimpered as I swallowed again the blade, sticky with snakes' blood.

"William," I whispered as desperation clawed at my insides. "Please don't do this."

His arm around me moved down, and William reached between my legs. Feeling a lack of undergarments and a distinct wetness, he made a sound of disgust in his throat. "You already let him *defile* you?" He made a gagging sound, and my cheeks heated with anger. "You burnt-arsed *whore*."

Yig hissed angrily, and his tail rattled menacingly where it was coiled beside him. "I'll give you one lassst chance, only because I don't wish to upset Essssie... Let her go."

"Call them off, or I'll kill her."

I begged. "William, *please–*"

"I'll tell everyone the snake god killed you. There'll be an outpouring of people killing snakes in revenge. You can't stop us *all*, Yig." William sneered, the curve of his cheek against my temple.

Yig said nothing, and the hissing around us increased. I could feel the bodies of hundreds of snakes moving around my legs, and William pressed the blade against my throat enough to draw a few droplets of blood.

I looked into Yig's eyes for reassurance he wasn't about to let me die, but his gaze was firmly set on William.

William's hand started to tremble.

The machete dropped from his fingers.

I took the opportunity to duck out from his hold, ran to Yig, and hid behind him as he stared William down.

"Wha–" William doubled over and clutched his stomach. The hissing intensified, and William screamed until I covered my ears from the agony of the sound. He collapsed to his knees and was immediately overrun by snakes. They moved across him, obscuring his body from view as his screams died down into unsettling gurgles that churned my stomach.

"Yig!" I grabbed Yig's arm, but he ignored me and continued to stare with his vertical pupils blown out at the writhing pile of his children.

The snakes started to dissipate and slid over and around my feet and Yig's tail as they returned to the forest quietly. Where William had fallen, lay a large black python, which curled itself into a defensive ball and tucked its head until its tail.

I stared.

"Is that…?"

"Yesss," Yig hissed, his lip curling into a smile. "You can send him home, where they will kill him, or…you can keep him as your pet." His lip curved further. "If you send him into the forest alone, my children will eat him alive."

My eyes widened, and Yig didn't stop me as I cautiously moved forward and knelt by the trembling python. When I touched its smooth skin, its head shot up to stare at me, its yellow eyes flecked with a deep brown.

But with round pupils. Human pupils.

"I didn't want this, but you *were* about to kill me," I whispered as I stroked its head. William the python continued to tremble, and eventually ducked its head against my palm. "Do you want to live with me? I'll keep you safe."

William glanced at Yig behind me as his shadow fell over both of us, before he looked at me. He didn't move or make to flee, so I scooped him up and let him wrap himself around my shoulders and arms, seeking warmth and comfort.

"Come," Yig said as he held his hand out, I took it, and William issued a low hiss, which Yig ignored. "When we get home, I'm going to fuck you in front of your new pet. First your cunt, then your asshole, then both at the same time." hHis gaze traveled to the python across my shoulders. "Later I'll *defile* you with your new toy's tail as you come. He may be your pet, but I will use him as I please to penetrate you."

My lip twitched into a smile, and I felt a twinge of guilt that disappeared as soon as I leant into Yig and allowed his scent to wash over me. Already I was anticipating the pleasure, and the ultimate release only Yig could give me. I would spread my legs for him and let him force both his members inside me until I screamed.

I wanted it all. I wanted everything he could give.

There was nothing else but this.

I was his now.

The legends of Yig continued amongst the locals and never lost their venom.

Added to the legends were sightings of a dark-haired woman who could be spotted briefly as she ran through the forest. Always barefoot, sometimes with her torn white dress flowing around her, other times naked as the day she was born. She was always laughing, and while Yig was never sighted, witnesses were certain if she was around, he wouldn't be far.

On occasion she had a large python draped around her shoulders and arms, and she'd simply stand at the threshold of where the trees ended and watch the daily life of people going by.

No one dared disturb or talk to her, and definitely made no attempt to bring her out of the forest and into civilization.

Legend says, a decade ago someone tried to take her away from the forest, and Yig cursed them to live the life of a snake.

But these were only legends, after all.

HEAT AND ICE

SERENA MOSSGRAVES

Have you ever seen your life flash before your eyes? My beloved and I have had a habit of getting out to the café once a week for the last fifteen years. We were mindless of the people around us; we had no idea there was anything to fear.

I regret none of my choices though.

I saw a glint of metal and didn't think. Grace was in danger and I couldn't stand the idea of what it would mean. Grace was thankfully quick to get me back to our house.

I felt the moment when I died and I wasn't ready to go yet. Decay is possible to be held back by the cold air. I found myself trying to find ways to stay with Elizabeth. Even staying in the house where it was cold took more energy than I had. I was grateful for her dedication to her work for the first time ever. She ordered groceries, not wanting to leave her studies, and I was so hungry. What possessed me I will never understand…

I invited the poor kid who delivered the groceries in. I didn't think it through. I tore into him ravenously. Thankfully, he was small, so I could hide the remainder of him before Grace came out. Eating him gave me a bit of energy. It also increased my hunger. I honestly wanted more. What was I becoming?

I found myself not wanting Grace to see the difference between the old me and the monster I became. I was terrified of losing the whole reason I was still here. She is not stupid though. She has to be told. I only hope she doesn't go mad at the idea of what I have become.

GRACE

Death was not going to steal from me the only woman I had ever loved. I found hints in old documents and I set up my home quickly. Though I need to control the temperatures of the room precisely, Elizabeth will survive. I will have to find the right mixture of proteins to keep her body functional. Perhaps I should organize my thoughts in this journal, and do so better than this horrific rambling I have scribbled thus far.

Elizabeth and I went for a walk in the beautiful city of New York. Heading to our favorite café—Café Thulu —for the treat of a latte and some crumble cakes. Two women in the big city don't usually draw attention. We made the same trip for around fifteen total years. Three from separate houses and twelve from the lovely little brownstone we bought in the city nearby together. I suppose our affection for each other angered the man who attacked us.

Elizabeth, foolishly, stepped in front of his knife. Most would have hurried her to the hospital, but I knew I had the supplies at home to care for her. I attended medical school. I don't trust hospitals. Most of the ones locally are run by money grubbers or ghouls. I stabilized her at the scene, hoping that would hold her until we made it home.

The air conditioning was as usual blowing cold air as I carried my beautiful girl into our room. I decided I would clean the sheets later. Elizabeth has always been one who preferred cooler temperatures.

Rushing about to gather what I needed, I noticed the blood trail. She had bled far more than one could and survive; realizing that, I hurried to her.

She smiled at me. "The cold made the pain stop, can we make it a little colder?"

The fear stole my breath away. I set the air conditioner as low as it could go and turned on every fan in the house. Then I worked on stripping her from the blood-soaked blouse. Normally, I would spend time lavishing those gorgeous titties with attention but the wound seeping blood on her side was more important.

The wound was not doing more than a light seep now, but the amount of blood that was soaked into her blouse and across our floor meant she should be dead. Pain was the body's way of telling us there was something wrong. So, if the cold made the pain stop… Well, I was going to make the house as cold as possible.

I recalled reading about experiments done to keep patients alive by lowering body temperatures and giving them transfusions. I did not know if I could get the necessary blood for transfusions. Maybe if I fed her protein she would heal. I would keep her wound clean. I would keep her comfortable. I only hoped I was wrong. My girl couldn't be dead.

I started working on studying everything I could find about the art of keeping the body alive in every way possible. Elizabeth asked for meat more than she had ever done before. I figured it was her body healing. The other thing was that her libido was also in overdrive. She was constantly asking me to touch her or feed her. Not that I minded either, except for the fact that it made it harder to figure out how to stop the wound from getting any worse.

The second day after the attack I was in my office, trying to read through the medical journals and she came in. I didn't hear her come into the room. Her hands seemed like they were stronger than usual as she started rubbing my thigh under my skirt. She was so rough, she put runs into my pantyhose.

"You are spending too much time with your books." Her voice was nearly a purr as her hands were already distracting my mind.

She slowly started working on removing my clothes, as she had been refusing to put anything on since she was injured. I had needed to wear more to be comfortable due to the temperature we had the house at. Her mouth roamed across my neck and nibbled at my ear. I no longer had the urge to ignore her. Giving in to her desire, I slowly started to kiss my way down the perfection of her body, promising myself I would return to the books after I saw to her needs. After all, she was the whole reason I was doing this, right?

She was so cold to the touch. I dared not change the air conditioner temperature, I suspected that was what was keeping her from passing on. Her desire to not damage any more of her clothes also made sense. She was always such a tidy woman.

Normally there was no part of her body I would not taste, but I avoided the spot where she was wounded. It was not even a conscious thing. It was just me unable to make myself look at the wound when we were in the middle of a heated moment.

After five days, even with the temperature being kept at nearly freezing in the house, I was beginning to smell a sickly sweet stench. I told her I needed to check the wound, offering to bathe her as a bribe. She was normally quite fond of bath play. Having my mouth lavishing attention on her pussy and breasts, having my fingers running through her hair. This was normally a turn-on for her. So it surprised me when she demurred away from the tub.

"Can't we just enjoy the bed? I don't want to take a bath right now. I just want to touch you. And I want your hands on me. I am not as worried about you licking me right now. I know I am not clean enough to make it enjoyable."

Now I was certain something was wrong. She enjoyed bathing and soaking in the water after our lovemaking. We had been together long enough that I was well aware of her tastes.

The smell reminded me of a bit of meat forgotten in the refrigerator. Something was rotting. The doctor in me knew I had to examine the wound whether she wanted me to or not. I found myself hesitating simply because I was in no hurry to confirm the truth I already knew.

Instead, I ordered groceries. Heavy on the meat. Then I went back to my books. When I came back out of my office, I found Elizabeth sitting in the kitchen, smiling. Though I had cleaned up the blood already from bringing her in, there was blood everywhere. Confused. I nearly stuttered out my surprise. "What did you do?'

"I ate. I put away the groceries you ordered. And I ate. You were so busy, I figured you would want me to take care of myself." She sounded so innocent, I couldn't fault her. Though I wondered where all this blood came from. I started to clean it up, telling myself that I did not want to know.

I had only been in my office for a couple of hours. I was both confused and finding that I wanted to become an ostrich about where the blood had come from, just bury my head in the same and ignore it. She seemed to no longer notice the blood and gore around her. I was happy to see she began to look more like herself, but I worried about that smell. The clothes she wore were light summer garments; in the temperatures of the house she should have been freezing. I had taken to wearing my heaviest of winter garments. I had the random thought that at least she was wearing clothing again.

I ran my hands across her arms looking for the goosebumps that should have been there. I felt none. Though I was obviously causing a reaction; she turned into my caress with a smile.

"So, are you done with the books for the evening?"

The excited tone of her voice made me feel like a jerk. No matter what else was going on, she was still my beloved. I pulled her in for a lingering kiss and lifted her gently to carry into our room. This time when I was kissing down her body, lingering slowly to lavish care first on one nipple, then the other, I slowly worked across her injured side. I was not going to be kissing the wound but I did want to get a look at it. This was the only way I figured she would let me look at it. I was glad I enjoyed our lovemaking with the lights on, for I sincerely doubted a change in routine would be a welcome thing in her current state.

Her coal-black hair spread across the pillows, covering them. Her skin was a porcelain painting that would burn if we spent any time in the sun. I loved watching the contrast with my dark skin. Her eyes were sapphires glistening in a heart-shaped face I had long since memorized. She often told me I was such an exotic dream to see. I looked in the mirror and I saw just another dark-skinned woman. She was the beautiful one between us. Though I know she felt the opposite was true. So often she had described me as being her midnight lover. She always claimed I had the intellect and beauty. Elizabeth was a poet.

Part of my worry was that since she was wounded, I had not seen her pick up the pen once. I swear she was fading away from me. I had no way to fix the situation. How could I be the intellect if I allowed her to die?

The wound had not healed. There was a scab of sorts, black and oozing a pus-like substance. Again I knew better than to put my mouth on the wound or the substance that slowly seeped around the scab. Didn't the fact that she was oozing pus mean she was still okay? The body only produces certain liquids while alive, right? I didn't want to worry Elizabeth, so I continued to kiss my way down to her gorgeous mound.

I spent time kissing her thighs before I turned my attention to her labia. I always took my time here. I felt my way through leaving the clit for the last. I wanted to memorize her body every time. She reveled in my slow and tender loving as though it was the only way it should ever be done.

We would have to address the wound. I would have to insist on it in the morning. I could let it be for tonight. That thought kept running through my head. I know that I was being a coward. The doctor in me said that she needed medicine. If I was unable to order it for delivery, I would have to go to the hospital. I knew the hospital was not likely to allow me to just take the medicine without the patient first being examined. She was not able to leave the house... I am not sure why but I felt like this was certain. If she left the cold then she would see the infection grow faster. I knew I was going to have to go, and I would have to be careful. I could only hope that she would listen and stay inside while I was gone.

The conversation the next morning almost surprised me. "I have no reason to leave the house today. I am comfortable. Though please return quickly. I will worry if you are gone for too long. I have grown used to being alone over the last few days as you spend your days in the office buried in your books. So, likely I will forget that you are not in there if you return quickly enough."

Elizabeth has always been something of a homebody, but when I went out she always wanted to go with me. This was not her normal behavior.

My fear at the idea I might not find her when I returned had me doing exactly as she asked. I hurried. I requested the most potent antibacterial and antibiotic drugs that I could get my hands on. The pharmacy staff merely checked my credentials and called the management to acquire permission to sell them to me. Though I had fears of paperwork stopping me, it seemed this process was going to be easier than expected. The permission was granted. Probably because I was not asking for any regulated drugs. I also bought some first aid supplies I knew I was low on and wound care supplies. These things I knew would come in handy when I cleaned the wound later on. Though I initially thought about giving her a transfusion, I admit that slipped my mind during the time and seeing the changes she was undergoing.

On my way home I made a stop at the grocers for a good sized lamb roast to make for dinner. Elizabeth had a fondness for lamb. I never tasted it before we started dating, but now it was something I tried to fix for her at least once a month. She often fixed food for me, and I was not as good a cook as she. I did not have her patience in the kitchen and would end up forgetting I had things cooking. The lamb was something I could put in the oven and set a timer for easily.

I felt like if I cooked her favorite meal tonight, maybe she would let me do what needed to be done. I was going to deal with the wound regardless of her desires, but I wanted her to not fight me on this. I had also, just in case, picked up a sedative while I was at the pharmacy. I just did not want to use it. All of this felt like I was taking away her consent. That felt so wrong. Life or death meant I was going to do what must be done...but I did not have to like the moral issues being raised in my brain.

The last stop before I went home was to the café for a take-out version of what we wanted the day she was injured. An iced latte for her with cinnamon crumble cake and a hot latte for me. I went for the blueberry crumble much as I always did. It felt good to purchase the same order. Most of the time, repetition was Hell. Only on occasion, Hell felt like home. It was someplace terrible but you felt too comfortable to ever leave.

The unknown can cut into the heart and leave the soul bare. I needed answers, and I was terrified of finding them. That thought had me picking up my pace and hurrying back to my beloved. I needed to know. I had to try to do something to stop the inevitable.

I was relieved to find her as I had left her. She was so excited to see me and pleased with the surprises I had brought that I felt extra bad for the delay. I should have been here at her side, not having an existential crisis over my own doubts. First I would have to take the proper time with my beloved, then I could do the medical necessities. She was obviously not going to die in the time it would take me to fix her dinner.

She was there as I was preparing the meal, chatting with her usual sunshine. I kept thinking about how lucky I was to have her in my life.

"I love you so much." I blurted suddenly.

She looked at me and smiled. "I love you too. Stop worrying about me."

I started to approach the idea right there but I guessed it was too much even for me. I dropped it and continued with the meal.

As per the usual, there was no lack of conversation with us. We were so well-suited for each other, similar interests and just enough difference to make the relationship interesting. We could have true discussions about things like books, music, movies, and the world at large.

When dinner was done, she had set our table. We worked well together. I was trying to keep from lapsing into an uncomfortable silence as we ate. I needed happiness. I don't know why I felt like that, but I did. I felt like if I let the moment slip away, everything would fall apart. I think I always knew what was going on.

After we ate, I coaxed her into the bedroom. I thought

about cleaning the wound first, or at least examining it. That was quickly dismissed. She was already irritable with my worry. I knew I needed her to be more relaxed and happy if I wanted to accomplish any of those tasks.

Instead of answering my questions, I spent time touching her as though I would never get to do that again. Starting with running my fingers through her long hair, untangling it and creating little braids. Then softly rubbing my thumbs across her delicate cheekbones and down to her lips. I was amused as she nibbled softly on my right hand as I was touching her face. This is the stuff that true memories are made of. The little moments where you and your beloved are the only ones existing in the universe.

Her skin was so cold, I felt like lava rubbing against ice. I leaned in for a kiss, capturing that thick bottom lip in between my teeth and holding it for just a moment.

Do you believe a moment can last forever? For me, that is what it felt like. I don't remember any sounds. I don't remember anything other than her. She was my entire thought process, all of my senses, and the only thing I ever wanted. Though we have lived in the same place for at least a dozen years, t. he entire time we have been together, at that moment I could not have described the room we slept in. I could not have told you what the house smelled like. Or any of the other things I should have been able to because all of my senses were overwhelmed with her.

As I started to kiss down her face, she pulled me back up for more of those deep kisses. Apparently, I was rushing it this time. I could handle that. Taking the cue from her behavior, I slowed myself down. I cannot explain how incredibly painful it is to go slowly when all you want to do is enjoy the beauty before you. I rubbed her nipples as I devoured her mouth. Feeling like I was falling into those sapphire wells she calls eyes. If I had been a religious woman I would swear I could see God in those eyes.

I knew at that moment, it wouldn't matter to me if she was dead or alive. As long as I could still have her in my life, nothing else mattered. I would still see if I could attend to her medically, but I was no longer panicked. She was still my Elizabeth. I would accept that, for whatever it was worth.

After we made the earth move, and I recovered my brains, I knew that the only way that I could look at myself in the mirror was to ask her. Then accept whatever choice she made. If that meant I couldn't heal her wound...well. I would have to accept that too. She deserved her boundaries. So, with a sigh, I asked her, "Elizabeth, my beloved, would you please allow me to attend to your side. It has an odor and I fear you may be getting worse."

She looked at me for an eternity, silent. When she

finally answered, it was only confirmation of what I already knew. "I am sorry, it would do no good. Grace, I died the same day I was injured. The cold air has kept me from decaying, but your medicine will not help me any further. I have remained because I could not stand the idea of leaving you."

Though I already suspected what she was telling me, and there was a part of me that was keeping my mind unaware that she could not yet live after losing so much blood...it hit me hard. I believe I went catatonic for at least a little while, as I blinked and she was sitting closer and worrying over me. I asked the only coherent thought I could manage to form. "Does this mean I am going to lose you?"

Reaching up and wiping the tears I did not realize were pouring from my eyes, she answered softly, "I don't know. When I first passed the cold was the only thing I had going to keep me alive. Since then, I have started to change. The sudden desire to eat things I would never have touched before... Well. Let's just say I think I will be okay. I am not going to heal and live as before, I think, but why does any of that matter? You still love me, don't you?'

My answer was immediate. "Of course I do! I honestly cannot imagine my life without you."

Her smile could light a city block. "Then do not worry about me. Let us just continue. When I am done changing, we will be able to go out again. I can feel it."

I can only hope she was right. I am done with this entry. I have my doubts as to whether I will ever want to revisit this journal again. However, if I am wrong...or if the worst happens...then this will serve as both a reminder and a record of events. May the elder gods forgive me. I no longer care what the outcome could be. I have my Elizabeth. That is all I will ever need.

THE DUNGEON

RAYNE MATTHEWS

Many years ago, there was a royal guard who told me I was of royal blood, and by the time I stopped laughing to ask questions, he was out of sight and refuses to speak to me to this day. If I were a royal descendant, I wouldn't be living in the dungeon as a worker. I'd be in the castle, living the best undead life, and more importantly, I wouldn't have to sneak around.

The dungeon isn't the worst place to be, most of the time.

I'm not obligated to socialize, fornicate, talk politics, or anything else the others have to do, day to day, but I miss it. Especially the fornicating part, because I was a sexual deviant in my previous life, even though they weren't always great experiences for me. I'm deeply in love with my forbidden, whom I sneak off to see in the woods, and I'm saving myself for him, although he doesn't seem as interested in me.

We live in the most beautiful kingdom, surrounded by water, and who doesn't love being around water? We do have to hold off the intruders from time to time, but my mother says they are no match for us because we protect the land, and the Old royal sea creatures protect the water.

It's a beautiful night and we're preparing for a fiesta to celebrate our King's birthday. No one really knows how old he is, but he doesn't look a day over thirty, so it's safe to assume he was fully turned around that age. We're a vampire coven and once we were turned to the "dark side," we were brought here to the island on the West Coast to live our days in peace away from humans and possible exposure. It makes no sense to me because vampires have been spoken about through the generations even being spotlighted in mainstream books and movies. Let me tell you, if *True Blood* or *Interview With The Vampire* were real, I would love to live in those worlds.

Now, there are different levels to vampirism, starting with the roamers, who live in the woods, and after being turned, the mix of their host's blood mutated, and they lost their humanlike characteristics. Most can still speak, but the others only make noises to communicate. The leader of the roamers is the one I sneak around with during the day when everyone is asleep.

How am I able to move around in the daylight? Another question I don't have the answer to because royals are the only ones who can do it, along with the roamers since their bodies took on the trait, so our king has put them on the frontlines for protection against our enemies.

Now, back to the roamers' leader. His name is Maxsimus, and just like the king's two sons, Jasper and Holden, he's beautiful. His mind is great, and I love to hear his stories about his life from before he was turned. He's over three hundred years old, and having a history lesson every time we talk is pure bliss for me.

My mother comes into our room in the dungeon with irritation. "Amalee, why are you not ready?"

"I don't think I want to celebrate tonight."

"You will not disrespect King Malloy on his special day."

"It's night, and it's not disrespectful. Look where we're kept, Momma. He doesn't care if we show up to his birthday party. I mean, who still has birthday celebrations at his age?"

"Quiet now. You will be ready and join. No more discussion."

She leaves, slamming the heavy door behind her, and I wish I hadn't been so vocal. Momma has done everything to be a good worker vamp, and I hate to hurt her feelings, but why does she care so much if I'm there for our king's party?

There are three royal families that make up our hierarchy, and since King Malloy's family are the only original vampires left, he and his offspring will remain at the top. For those asking, according to history, our King was the first who was born a vamp, and the powers he possesses came from a host who is still unknown, but if I'm being honest, I don't understand the politics behind it. You get bitten and turn into a vampire, or you're mutated to become a roamer. That's all that makes sense to me, and I hate having to think about a more complex scenario into what we are. Obviously, someone had to have gotten bitten to make us the "indestructible" creatures we are.

I'm in the pretty dress Momma made for me, then go out to the main court of the kingdom, and it's beautiful. I don't know where they got balloons, but if it's what our king requested it's not surprising to see.

"Amalee, where have you been?" my best friend Amina asks, rushing over to give me a hug. She's a lighthouse vamp, and it's a major step up from us dungeon dwellers, and they work directly for the royal servants in the castle.

"I don't think I like this."

"What?"

"A party. King Malloy is like a million years old. Why a celebration like this?"

"Because he can. Have you seen Maxsimus?"

"It's been a few days. I've seen him staring at the dungeon and I should probably see him soon."

"He doesn't question why you can walk around during the sunlight hours?"

"No. He'd rather keep our conversations light-hearted."

"I saw a roamer last night around the gates."

"They're supposed to protect us, so that's not uncommon."

"He was sniffing."

"Sensing danger, maybe?"

"Maybe. I have to tell you something and you can't get mad at me."

"It takes a lot to get me mad."

"I went to Prince Holden's room."

The perk up of my body is highly recognizable. "Did you have sex with him?"

"Would you be mad if I said yes?"

"You did? How was it?"

"Horrible. He drooled all over me like a dog."

"Gross. You remember how dogs act?"

"I only remember the one I had when I was young, and he drooled all the time."

"I'm sorry that happened. I guess royals aren't so perfect after all."

"I guess not. After the party, would you like to come up to my room and watch TV?"

"I'd love to. We have to keep up with current events, so we don't talk like we're old."

"Agreed. Do you think we'll marry one day?"

"You will. I'm a dungeon vamp. We're forbidden to be happy."

"I think it's fucked."

"Amina. Don't curse so loudly."

"I don't care."

"Me either, but the guards could hear you and neither of us need to be punished."

"Yeah, you're right. Let's see what else we need to do."

The only hope is for things to run smoothly because the last thing we need is to get into trouble with one of the royals.

The party is profoundly ridiculous because King Malloy has requested every vamp to approach his decorated throne to say one thing about him we're grateful for, and now I'm next.

Just wonderful.

Queen Rubia motions for me to take my place in front of King Malloy, and he's staring at me with his normal blank expression.

"Amalee. What have you to share?" he asks, taking a sip from his goblet.

I do the usual lady curtsey, lowering my head the way I was taught. "Happy birthday, my Lord. I am grateful for your patience and willingness to allow us dungeon dwellers to be amongst the royals."

He turns his head, and I do believe I know an eye

roll when I see one, but I wait for his acceptance of my words.

"Are you satisfied in the dungeon, Amalee?"

"It's better than living in the woods, I suppose."

"Where would you rather rest your head?"

"Is this a real question, my Lord?"

"I've asked it, haven't I?"

"Sorry. The castle would be a dream come true."

"It will be considered."

"My Lord?"

"Honesty is a trait I respect."

"Thank you, my Lord."

Another curtsey, and I walk quickly in bewilderment, bypassing my mother serving food to find Amina, glad to not get yelled at by one of the royal guards as if I'm some wild teenager who needs a spanking.

Wait, are teenagers allowed to get spanked anymore?

I love how the ones around here see me as a vibrant young person, but I'm older than most of them in our undead state, but I don't go around bragging about being a hundred and six.

The biggest secret this kingdom holds is me and who my father is. My mother was a human, King Malloy turned her when she was twenty-five, but I was born a vampire, which only happens for royal babies.

Malloy bit me on my twenty-first birthday, releasing my full potential, but I had to take an oath to never tell anyone. I don't know why, since he is in control of who is chosen to be turned and join our coven, and I'm positive it has everything to do with the reason Momma is forbidden to speak to our king.

My theory is they had an affair, and his wife didn't like it. It's the only plausible answer, but again, it doesn't matter because I am a dungeon vamp, so I have no choice but to keep quiet.

As for how our species can make babies… Males can as long as it's with an unturned woman. For obvious reasons, once women turn we can no longer conceive. In all honesty, it would be a madhouse if we could, especially because we stop aging. Oh, and if you're not born a royal, the sun will be your greatest enemy.

Amina is nowhere to be found, so I go into the lighthouse, and the closer I get to her room, I hear familiar noises. Someone is partaking in the act of sex, and I'm nosy enough to find out who it is, but I stop outside her cracked door, and it's confirmed this is where it's coming from, and when I peek in, my temperature rises.

Prince Holden stands with his knees slightly bent as a royal servant sucks glorious dick. I shouldn't be referring to his penis as such, but it sounds better in the situation.

It's so big it puts the others I had before turning to shame, but what's making me hot is how he's holding Amina's hips in place, with her top half bent back, to where she's completely upside down, licking her clit furiously, and now I understand why the noises were heard so far away from the door.

Passing up a prime masturbation opportunity is out of the question, so I look around to make sure it's safe, then lift my dress, slipping a hand into my panties, lubing my finger, and circle my clit. The last thing I need is to get caught, but how exciting would it be, as long as it's not by my mother.

With my eyes closed, I take in Amina's moans, hyper focused on my stimulation, and I'm almost there when I feel a presence in front of me, and I'm half horrified when I open my eyes.

"What are you doing, Amalee?"

"I'm sorry, Prince Holden."

"Are you enjoying yourself?"

"Yes."

"Come in." He takes my hand from my panties, and puts my index and middle fingers into his mouth. "You are exquisite."

I've never been called exquisite before and it hits a little deeper since Holden is a royal, but I'm not shy, and whatever is about to happen, I will be a willing participant. Even if he's a drooler, it's been decades since I've had any type of sexual encounters with another, and it's time to end the celibacy.

Holden leads me to the bed, lifting my dress, and the servant girl pulls my panties down, then softly pushes me back onto the firm mattress.

Amina positions herself behind me, massaging my breasts over my dress, and presses her mouth to my ear. "I've wanted you for a long time, Amalee."

My body shivers with excitement because I too have always wanted to know what she tastes like, and not only in a sexual way. Her blood calls for me every time we're alone, and now is my chance to find out.

Blood mixing between lovers is incredibly erotic and it brings us some type of euphoria that makes us lose our undead minds. Now that I think of it, it's probably the reason Holden drooled all over Amina, and it means her blood is magically delicious.

I turn my head to look her in the eyes, and it's so sexy to see them bright green. It means she's turned on and I'm sure my eyes already match, especially when Holden pushes the servant girl onto her knees between my legs.

"Service her."

She doesn't say a word, and the hunger radiates from her body as she dives in tongue-first, connecting with my clit, and I don't hold back on showing how good it feels with loud moans.

"Amina. I wanna taste you."

Her hunger matches the servant's, and she moves to my side resting one leg under my head, and the other on my bent knee. "You have no idea how long I've been waiting for this."

Before I lick her, I align my fangs just above her clit, to show how much I want her, and when I sink my fangs in she thrashes, moaning crazily.

Holden seems to be left out of the situation, and I pull my fangs out of Amina when he turns me onto my side and sinks his massive hardness into me. It's been so long, and it feels amazing. Sure, I'm more into Jasper who's his brother, but if this is the scenario in front of me, then I'm all for it.

"Does that feel good, Amalee?" Holden asks between moans.

"Oh yes."

Before I completely give my sanity over to bliss, I press my mouth against Amina's clit and suck with enough pressure to make her see stars, but with her head back, I can't see the look on her face, and I'm not sad about it as she grinds her hips, moaning so loud I'm sure a lot of our coven can hear her from outside. Not likely, but it would make me happy to know they knew someone was getting pleasured properly.

As my orgasm takes its time building, a set of fangs puncture my breast, and just like that, I explode into a million pieces, but once my vision clears, Holden is staring at me with the most shocked look on his face, and he's immediately soft inside me.

"Your blood."

"What about it?"

He gets up, giving his servant a direct order to gather his clothes and they rush out of the room before I'm able to process what happened.

What's wrong with my blood?

CHAPTER THREE

It's been a few days since my romp with Amina, Holden, and the servant girl, and he clearly told King Malloy, because I was informed I would not be moving into the castle. I can't explain what happened in Amina's room after our prince bit me, but he's avoiding me as if I have an infectious disease and, every time I try to get his attention, a guard turns me away. To make matters worse, Amina and my mother are being short with me, and I feel terrible.

To get my mind off of things, I get up before sunrise to make sure everyone is asleep, then make my way into the woods to visit Maxsimus.

The roamers live pretty deep in the woods near the ocean, in rundown cottages the royals built many generations ago, and I've always been curious as to why, but my nosiness isn't that great, so I never ask.

I knock on the door, and my breath gets caught in my throat when he opens it wearing nothing at all.

"Oh, Amalee. Good to see you."

He makes no attempt to cover himself, so I take in his lower half until he ruins my view by putting both hands over his delightful gift.

"Good morning, Max. Is this a bad time?"

"No. You may come in."

"Thank you. Are you heading to bed, or just getting up?"

"Neither."

Before he closes the door a female roamer who is also nude runs past us, picking up the pace once she's outside, and I shake my head, laughing. "I see."

"What did you think we did out here?"

"I don't know, I guess I never thought about sex being involved."

"You think because of the way we look, we don't fornicate?"

"Like I said, I never thought about it. Can you make yourself decent, please? I have to talk to you and I can't be distracted."

His half-smile exposes a fang, and I imagine how he looked before he was mutated. Maxsimus is a show stealer, and females of any species would line up to spend time with him in a sexual way. I know because I'm one of them, and as he walks away, I take in what I can of his ass, but it's too dark in here to be successful, so I sit on a chair, resting my elbows on the small table.

He comes back with pants on and occupies the other chair. "What is it, Amalee?"

"I wasn't gonna tell you, but there's no one else I can talk to."

"Go on."

"I'm sure you know King Malloy's birthday was the other day, but I partook in sexual things."

"With Malloy?"

"No. Prince Holden."

"Do you feel guilty?"

"No, but when he bit me, he said *your blood*, and ran out. What could be wrong with my blood?"

"Nothing. A century's old mystery has been solved."

"What does that mean?"

"He has confirmed you are a royal."

"How would he confirm that?"

"Royal blood tastes the same. He recognized it, and I have a hunch he wasn't pleased."

"There's no way I'm actually a royal."

"Explain how you can walk in the sunlight."

"Okay, but which family am I a part of?"

"I do not have the answer to that." He slides his chair closer to me, taking my hand. "There is an old tale of a lost royal child, but it was never said as to whose child it was."

"There's no way I could be King Malloy's daughter, right?"

"I do not know."

"The extended royal families were born vamps, right?"

"I believe so."

"You know something, Max. Why won't you tell me?"

"There are many things I know, but if you want answers you must speak with the descendants of Cthulhu."

"What would they know?"

"They are the Old royals of the sea."

"Don't I have to offer something to talk to them?"

"Correct."

"What should I offer?"

"Your body."

"That's forward."

"Indeed."

"Will you go with me?"

"I cannot. They prefer to have women without onlookers."

"Wonderful. I didn't have sex with sea creatures on my to-do list for today."

"I believe it will be better than the experience you had with Holden."

His half-smirk makes me laugh, but I'm nervous about this and need to think it through because I've heard many things about the descendants of Cthulhu, and they've become well known for taking women of all species to satisfy their sexual cravings. A few light-house vamps went missing some years ago and the royal guards found them with the sea dwellers, but refused to leave, so whatever it is they're doing in the water must be something good if the ladies fought tooth and nail to stay with them.

Maxsimus stares at me with his neon blue eyes, and I love when he looks at me this way. Most people would run away to see a roamer, but I see the true beauty in the mutation. They don't look old or scary to me with their worn appearance and I wish they could live among us, at least in the dungeon because I feel they are more useful on the castle grounds then out here in the woods.

What I love the most is how gentle they are. Maybe they were this way before being turned, but even the ones who can no longer form words communicate through sounds or gestures and it always makes me feel safe. Now, the cutest part is their ears. During the mutation their ears shrunk, almost shriveled up and they're so small, but Maxsimus gives me Hell whenever I try to play with them.

I move over, and he doesn't complain when I sit on his lap, interlacing my fingers behind his neck. "You know, I could skip the descendants and offer my body to you for information."

"You couldn't withstand what I have to offer, Amalee."

"Would you care to put a wager on it?"

"No."

"So you think I can't handle it? Before I was fully turned, I was considered a sex addict."

"Craving sex is nothing compared to what I need to be satisfied."

"Then why don't we try?"

"You mean too much to me."

"You're so sweet, Max, but I promise I can take it. I'd probably like it."

The tensing of his body confuses me until I look into his eyes, and the shift in him isn't from lust. He's as sincere as they come, and I need to be satisfied with what we have, so I move back to the other chair, and he relaxes a little.

"I'm sorry, but I cannot engage in those things with you."

"I understand. You know I'm only joking around, right?"

"You are not, but as I said, you mean too much to me."

"I should get some sleep."

I get up to make a clean getaway, but Maxsimus grabs my wrist gently, making me stop to face him.

"I love you, Amalee."

"I love you too. I'll come see you tomorrow."

"You don't have to go. You can sleep here."

"Will you hold me close?"

"Yes. I will never hurt you."

"And I'd never hurt you, Max. Let's go to sleep."

We walk side by side to his bedroom, and I'm given a robe to wear, so I'm comfortable out of my dress, then we lay on his bed, falling asleep peacefully with me in his arms.

I know Maxsimus cares for me deeply and it's the reason he won't take things further, but I wish we could be so much more. He's a lot older than I am, and in his many years, he's cemented himself as someone who doesn't cross the line with those he loves, which I respect, but if he would give us a chance, I think we could be an amazing couple.

Until then, I'll try to behave myself.

CHAPTER FOUR

When we wake, it's close to sunset, and Maxsimus walks me to the edge of the woods leading to the castle grounds. We quickly say our good-byes so I can get back to the dungeon before everyone wakes from their slumber.

The best part of spooning with Maxsimus is how he tries his damndest to conceal the erection he gets from being with me, and make no mistake, I don't help the situation. A little wiggle of my ass against him usually ends with me giggling uncontrollably and him speaking one of the many languages I do not, which is sexy to hear since it's so foreign to my ears because I'm originally from Georgia and before I met King Malloy, I had never known anyone outside of the area I lived.

Strange enough, Malloy was always coming around when I was a little girl, and Momma did the best she could to prepare me for what I would become once I was deemed ready, and it makes sense I'm a royal descendant since our king always told me I was special in the same way he is. Do I think he's my father? I don't know, but even if he is, it doesn't change anything I did with Holden.

As vampires, our sexual cravings are powerful, and group activities in a sexual manner isn't unheard of, blood relation or not. I was forbidden to engage in the act with someone else because Momma didn't like my behavior before I was fully turned, especially since I was sleeping with older men as a teenager. Why would I go after a boy my age who has no experience? I've always known exactly what I want in a lover since I was young, and being celibate for so long was excruciating. Now I can open up and have as much pleasure as I desire. Male or female. Maybe even a sea creature.

As everyone gets up to start working, I leave the dungeon to find Amina, who is washing a sheet near the edge line of the cliff, overlooking the ocean.

"Hey."

She jumps, spinning to face me. "I'm so mad at you."

"What did I do?"

"I was having so much fun, then you made Holden run off with his servant."

"I'm sorry, I was surprised too."

"Okay, I'm not mad at you. I'm mad it ended that way."

"I'm sorry."

She takes my hand, pulling me in for a squeeze, and kisses my cheek. "I love you and I'm sorry too. What did he mean about your blood?"

"Maxsimus said all royal blood tastes the same."

"So you're a royal?"

"Maybe."

"It makes sense since you're not a roamer and can walk around during the day."

"What if I'm Malloy's daughter?"

"Queen 'pole up her ass' will throw a fit."

"I know. Do you think I should talk to him?"

"If he allows it, but you can't talk to him around her."

"True. Maxsimus also said if I want answers, I have to offer my body to the sea descendants."

"That sounds fun."

"I tried to act like I wasn't into it, but it does sound fun."

"Take me with you? If there are two of us, they can't deny the information."

"They come onto land before sunrise, so I don't think that's a good idea."

"Then how did all those other vamps stay alive?"

"I don't know. I'll go while everyone meets for King Malloy's words before bed."

"Perfect timing. Everyone will be napping, so they won't notice."

"Exactly. Have you ever met anyone besides him who loves the sound of his own voice so much?"

"My father was like that and it's a turn off."

"I agree. At least he's handsome and his voice isn't bad."

"Still puts me to sleep."

We giggle, and I help her finish up with the sheet, hanging it on the dry line, then we go up to her room in the lighthouse to watch TV until we're called upon.

There are endless things on the TV to keep us entertained that we didn't have a century ago. We didn't have televisions or radios before we came here, only the newspaper and books because we were dirt poor, so it's nice to watch scripts or a true story being acted out in front of you to get a better visual of what's going on.

The technology this world has is amazing and I wonder how we have it all, considering humans are usually the ones who install it. We're far away from any mainland, and when planes or helicopters are overhead, they are dealt with by the royal guards, and it's the scariest thing to hear. The booms from their weapons are loud and even make the ground shake, but our king feels it's necessary because humans don't need to know who and what lives here.

"Human nature seems so violent," I blurt out.

Amina shifts to face me. "There is bad in any form, Amalee. What's important when we watch these stories is to be educated and not get ourselves in the same situations.”

“I know, but it seems so senseless. I know we aren’t the best when it comes to violence against humans, but we need it to survive. Hurting someone for fun is wrong.”

“I think they’d say the same thing about us. Don’t act like you don’t enjoy the taste of human blood.”

“I’m not saying that at all. Never mind.”

“You think too much. You broke your celibacy, so focus on that.”

“Momma is gonna murder me when she finds out.”

“You need to stop letting her control your life. Before you were turned, you were an independent adult.”

“I try to tell her that, but I’m her only child, so she hovers.”

“She needs to have sex.”

“You think she doesn’t? I’ve seen her doing it with a few of the royal guards.”

“No!”

“Yes.”

“Is that where you get your appetite from?”

“I don’t think so. She says it’s from my father.”

“The father she won’t reveal?”

“That’s the one. I have a feeling the answers will come sooner than later.”

"This place will burn to the ground if it turns out you're the king's offspring."

"I know. Is it bad that I want to see the chaos?"

"No. I wanna see it too."

More giggles and we get back to the show on the TV, but before it ends, a guard comes in telling us I've been summoned to the king's quarters. His quarters is his bedroom and normally he meets in the formal room to address any of us, so I'm more curious than scared. Whatever King Malloy has to say, he doesn't want anyone to hear it.

But, if this isn't the perfect opportunity for me to ask as many questions about where I came from, I don't know what is.

Walking into the castle is always mentally and visually stimulating because every window is tinted by beautiful stained glass with every color imaginable, but it's always bright inside. The light is more than the lightbulbs in the endless chandeliers aligning the ceilings, and when the guard knocks on the door to King Malloy's room, it opens showing our Lord.

"Amalee, come in." He turns his focus on the guard. "We are not to be interrupted."

"Yes, my Lord."

The door closes and we're alone, making me nervous because our king never lets on to what he's thinking until he speaks.

"Have you bathed, Amalee?"

"Before sunrise, my Lord."

"Excellent. Remove your clothing and lie on the bed."

What?

Going against our king's instruction does not go unpunished, so I take my dress and panties off, and lie on the large bed, on my back. "My King?"

"Yes, my darling?"

"Why do I have to be naked? Am I being unannounced?"

Unannounced is his version of punishment.

"Absolutely not. Holden informed me of your doings, and I want to witness it myself."

"What do you mean?"

He sits on the bed next to me and puts a gentle hand on my stomach. "You will soon see, my darling."

"Why are you calling me your darling?"

"You are."

"Am I your daughter?"

"Silly girl. You will do as I ask."

"Yes, my Lord."

The door opens and our queen steps in looking disgruntled. "What is this, Malloy?"

"My love, this is an offering."

I know what an offering is amongst vamps, and sex is involved, so I sit up, pushing out my breasts to entice her. I ended my celibacy and I'm in full sex mode. Queen Rubia is the worst, but she's gorgeous, and I don't hesitate to help her when she stands next to the bed, and begins undressing.

"My Queen."

"Amalee. Are you a predator or prey?"

"Predator."

"Good. I love being chased."

I hope she understands what this means, because I will not hold back, and our King will probably have me executed if I don't keep myself under control.

After she climbs onto the bed, I push her down with more force than intended, spreading her wide before looking at our king, who has removed his trousers, sitting with a fistful of his manhood. I see being well endowed runs in the bloodline.

"Is this what you want, my Lord?"

"Yes."

That's all I need and once I'm on my belly, I swipe my tongue from ass to her clit, making her moan, and her pussy is hands down the best I've tasted. No wonder King Malloy took her as his bride and made two gorgeous princes in the process.

Queen Rubia thrashes around like a maniac as I circle my tongue around her clit, and I lower one of her legs to have a full view of our king, to watch him pleasure himself as he makes eye contact with me with a smirk on his face.

I never thought I would be summoned to the king's quarters to screw his wife, but I'm not at all complaining, and the way he's admiring me between her legs, I lift up onto my knees and rub my clit wildly to finish at the same time she does. It doesn't take long for her to reach down, grasping my hair tightly, and I continue my assault until she lets go, but I have more work to do. I move over to the edge of the bed with my legs wide, and keep the fast pace with enough pressure, not taking my eyes away from him until we come simultaneously.

What a rush.

As if they were waiting at the door, the king's head servant comes in and cleans each of us, starting with Malloy, and I keep my legs wide after she leaves.

"You didn't join us, my Lord."

"This was for you and my bride, my darling. Are you satisfied?"

"Yes."

"Excellent. We will call upon you again."

"I can't wait, my king."

"Dress and tend to your duties."

"As you wish."

They watch me dress, and I'm all smiles as I walk out of the castle down to the worker vamps and ask a royal guard what needs to be done. By the way he's sniffing around me, he knows what I've been up to. It turns me on to see his hooded eyes as if he wants to pull me away for some play, but I gather my wits and join the others near the cliff to help wash.

Things are going great with everyone laughing and

having a good time when my arm is forcefully pulled back, and I'm a little surprised my mother is being so aggressive, and I'm ready to give her a piece of my mind when we go into the dungeon and she slams the door.

"What the fuck are you doing, Amalee?"

"What is your problem?"

"You went to his room and came out here smelling of disgusting lust."

"How dare you? I am a grown woman and whatever I am asked to do by our king I will do. Isn't that what you taught me?"

"He will only use you, and when he's done, he will throw you off the cliff to the sea creatures."

"Then so be it. You're jealous he's showing me attention and not you."

She's quick to throw her arm back, and I catch her by the wrist before she connects with my face, and her eyes go wide.

"Amalee."

"Don't. I'm tired of you controlling every aspect of my life. I am living for me now, and there's nothing you can do about it."

"You've had relations. You know what it will do."

"If you ever try to strike me again, I will drag you out at sunrise and watch you perish."

"It's already happening."

"Get out."

"You'll regret trusting him."

The look of sadness washes over her face, identical to mine, and when she storms off, I give chase, realizing my mistake. Grabbing her arm, I pull her in for a hug.

"I'm so sorry, Momma."

"Oh, Amalee. You're all I have left."

"Please forgive my words?"

"I will always forgive, my little rainbow."

"I love you."

"I love you too."

"Can I tell you something?"

"Of course."

"I've been going into the woods and visiting with a roamer."

"Why?"

"He's brilliant, Momma, and I love him."

"You will take me to him."

"For what?"

"I knew you were going out there, so I must meet him. My daughter will not marry a degenerate."

"Marry? He doesn't see me as a partner."

"We'll see."

It's always been this easy, and making up with Momma feels great, but her meeting Maxsimus is an entirely different storm. If she doesn't like him, she will not hesitate to lock me up at sunrise, so I don't sneak off, but what if she meets him and steals him away?

CHAPTER SIX

I feel as if I'm losing my mind. There's no mistaking I'm in a sexual lust haze, and as I sit at the waterline of the ocean, all I want is for the sea creatures to take me away to pleasure island with no estimated time of return.

Before I was officially turned, Malloy allowed me to act on my urges and I slept with many men, who I now know were vampires, but it wasn't until the day Malloy turned me that a new sexual hunger was unleashed. Momma was the angriest I've ever seen, and she forbade me of any sexual behaviors, other than an occasional masturbation, and for decades, I was successful.

With my eyes closed, head resting on my bent knees, you can imagine the shock when I'm suddenly pulled under the water. The gasp wasn't a sufficient intake of breath and if I don't get air, there will be a dead dungeon vamp on their hands, and even though I can't open my eyes, I know what's taken me is a descendant of Cthulhu.

They're the largest living sea creatures, and if I'm being honest, when they come onto land, they win that trophy as well. The octopus-like face is unnerving the first time you catch a glimpse, but if you want to keep your sanity, you shouldn't stare for too long because eventually you'll lock eyes. These are rumors, since I've never met anyone who went mad from making eye contact, but it's best to be safe than sorry.

Just before I'm out of breath and drown, I'm lifted above water and set onto the most beautiful rock formation overlooking the ocean. I wish I weren't struggling to fill my lungs to enjoy it, but it's still gorgeous.

The descendant is leaning on the edge next to me and I look everywhere else but his eyes. I know it's a male because they have differences in appearance than the females.

"I'm Amalee."

"What troubles you?"

I didn't look him in the eyes, so there's no way I'm going mad, but his voice booms in my head with a touch of gentleness.

"I was told you can answer my questions for a price."

"An offering is necessary."

If I had to guess, he's one of the younger descendants and it makes me smile because I've heard the older ones are grumpy.

"Are you allowed to share secrets of King Malloy?"

"Yes."

"Am I his daughter?"

"What do you offer?"

"What's a suitable offering to you?"

"Loyalty brings freedom."

Before I have the opportunity to answer, another creature emerges from the water and climbs up the rock, settling next to me. This one is different, but not a female. The fish-like appearance along with scales along its neck tells me it's a loyal follower of the descendants, but I'm not sure why it's here.

I refocus on the larger creature's chest, resting my hands on my lap. "I'm not sure what you mean by loyalty brings freedom, but I need answers."

"Very well."

It's evident, these two can speak to each other without me hearing and I won't lie and say I'm not turned on when the descendant lifts me with one hand and the other swipes his unrealistically large tongue under my dress, pulling my panties off in a less than subtle way, but it doesn't bother me. Fornicating is what I need and although I've never been with anyone or anything other than a human or vamp, it will definitely make for a good story.

I have to remember I'm here for answers and not

pleasure, but mixing the two seems justifiable, so I take their lead, and after my dress is removed I'm filled by the follower and oh boy, I'm not disappointed, and when the descendant presses himself against my ass, I tense, clenching my butt cheeks. There is no way in any world that thing is fitting inside of me, but after he spreads me and begins pushing in, it gets smaller.

How is this possible?

When he's fully in, it's still entirely too large, but not hard like all of my other experiences. It's kind of squishy, but with a desirable purpose.

I'm in erotic heaven. Even more so when I'm flipped over and they switch holes making me scream in true pleasure, as I do my best to gain the right motion to feel them both to the max. Thankfully, it works, and the screeching from them means I'm doing everything right.

The worst part is when your partner or partners finishes before you, and this is obviously happening now, as they both tense up like cement and I'm lifted off of the descendant like a fire hydrant exploding.

I hope this was enough to get my answers.

The descendant lifts me off of their penises and rests me onto his chest. *"You will have your answers , Amalee."*

"Don't you need to know my questions?"

"You have asked."

"Oh. Right. What now?"

"We will bathe, and you may return to your dwelling."

"Thank you."

The other creature licks my face and jumps off of the rock into the water, and all I want is to sleep, but the descendant lifts me like a newborn and lowers us into the water, and I'm grateful he doesn't try to drown me again.

The tide is high, but with him being so tall and large, it's no issue, so I maneuver around, still on his arm, to watch the waves crash against the rock. The sound of the rough seas used to scare the life out of me because drowning was always my biggest fear, and even though it could've happened today, I take comfort in the sounds knowing the Descendant will not drop me.

It's nearing sunrise and it's been hours since I left the royal grounds, so when we're done he hands me my dress, and walks me back to shore, setting me down so the waves only come up to my knees.

"You are the heir to the throne."

I don't know if I want to pass out or die, but either is inviting.

"What?"

"You will rule the coven."

"I-I am Malloy's daughter?"

"Yes."

And with that, he walks away, disappearing into the water, and I'm stuck standing in shock, clutching my dress to my stomach.

The descendants do not lie, so it explains why Holden was so upset when he tasted my blood. I'm older than him and Jasper, so it would more than likely mean neither will ever be king.

I hear my name being yelled, snapping me out of my stunned demeanor and I'm thankfully dressed by the time a royal guard approaches.

"Amalee, you are not permitted to leave the grounds without permission."

"I wanted to swim."

"King Malloy wants to see you at the gathering."

"What? Why?"

Without saying another word, he does an overdramatic about-face and begins his walk back out of the woods, and I'm scared. The gathering is the place where Malloy lays down the law for our coven, so I'm not exactly thrilled to be the center of attention there. At least it's almost sunrise and the entire coven won't be witnesses to what he'll do. It is semi embarrassing because the princes will, but I can't think about it because I need to get back to the grounds before the secrets are revealed. Me being a royal is or should be a good thing, but I've enjoyed being without responsibility.

My stupid, childish ways of thinking are ripped away when I get to the gathering and see the royals surrounded around the only person I can't imagine not having in my life.

CHAPTER SEVEN

Jasper and Holden are restraining my mother, and it hurts my once beating heart more because she isn't fighting against their entrapment, but there's nothing I can do since the attention is on the guards and Queen Rubia rushing into the castle for shelter, but I have to save my momma. The sunlight will kill her and I'm at a loss trying to figure out why she's being punished.

Malloy steps before me, looking up at the sky. "Daylight is upon us."

"Why is my momma out here?"

"Why were you away from the grounds?"

"I needed questions answered. Let her go inside and I'll tell you."

"No need, my darling. Are you satisfied with your answers?"

"No."

"No?"

"No. Stop wasting time and let her go inside."

"It pains me to punish my only daughter, but you will conform to the life I've given you, or you will be unannounced."

He's punishing me by taking my mom away, and reality hits me harder than anything I've felt before. I can't lose her, and crying isn't something vamps do often, but the tears pour out of the eyes faster than the waves were rolling in on the beach.

"Please don't take her away. I should be the one being punished."

"You are being punished."

"You think if you dust her, I'll conform?"

"I know you will. Who else would you have? Maxsimus isn't a proper companion."

The reaction is involuntary, and I should've been more careful since he and the other born royals can walk around freely during the times I sneak off, but this isn't right.

"Please, my Lord. You made me with her."

"She was only the vessel to birth my child. A boy is what you should have been."

"Then why did you fully turn me?"

"You attended school alone from the first year to the last and I was pleased with your progress."

"You're talking gibberish now. Let her go."

He looks up at the sky again and smiles. "The time has come, Amalee."

"I won't let you kill her because you're too selfish."

"I am many things, but selfish is not one."

"You are a piece of shit."

With all of my strength, I take in as much air as I can and scream. This is something Maxsimus instructed me to do if I needed help, and it works. I didn't know I had the lung capacity to do it so loudly, but before we all know it, there are roamers surrounding us.

Malloy looks around with a grin. "I see he's taught you some valuable lessons."

Before I can open my mouth to respond, the first ray of sunshine peeks through the clouds above and Momma screams in pain as her arms begin to burn, so I rush over to the princes.

"Please let her go."

"You should have followed the rules," Jasper says in a barely audible tone.

"If you let her die, I will seek revenge. You know what that means, right?"

If there's one thing about them is how loyal they are to each other, and without looking at the other to confirm, they let Momma go, and a roamer rushes over, picking her up, and with lightning speed, runs into the woods. I feel a little better because the trees will provide enough shade until she's taken inside.

But what I don't expect is for Malloy to grab my

wrist, pull me over to a covered table we use for blood letting of animals that are hunted, and strap my arm to it above my wrist. I'm sure he will drain me to death, but this is a strange way to restrain me.

His intention is answered as Maxsimus approaches and Malloy pulls his beloved knife from its sheath, and without warning, he drives the blade into the middle of my wrist, then in one swift motion, drags it through my hand until it's free.

My screams are so loud, I'm not sure if I can stay standing much longer, and our king surprises me once again by lifting his knife and bringing it down with force, removing my four fingers and half of my thumb.

"Malloy, enough."

The pain is unbearable, but Maxsimus' voice seems to do the trick, and I may be on the verge of unconsciousness. I feel there is more to the story between the king and the roamer, but why didn't Maxsimus try to stop him?

"Punishment complete. Get this betrayer off my grounds," Malloy says, walking away, motioning for his sons to follow.

Maxsimus rushes to my side, releasing my arm, and picks me up, taking me into the woods. "You've lost a crucial amount of blood. You must feed, Amalee."

I wish I could speak, but the pain has turned to numbness, eliminating the usage of my vocal cords. And when we get into Maxsimus' domain, my only agenda is to take care of my mom, who's sitting on the floor, curled up into herself, rocking back and forth as she cries. I don't care about my injury because she needs me more, so I give a little fight against Max's hold and he sets me down, so I can be by her side.

When I touch her foot with my uninjured hand, she looks up with tears streaming down her cheeks, but the second she realizes it's me, she does what any great mother would do. She forgets about her own pain and begins checking my body for wounds, and instead of going insane seeing my hand, she gives the roamers clear instructions, then applies pressure to my hand with her dress.

"Oh, my little rainbow. I'm so sorry."

The words won't come out, so I press my forehead to hers, avoiding the burns which start at her temple and cry. I still can't feel the pain or anything from my wrist to where my fingers once were, but Maxsimus is right in saying I need to feed because I'm still losing a lot of blood, and the worst case scenario is bleeding out. Amputating my hand isn't the easiest to stomach, but it's what needs to be done or I will die.

An hour ago, I was in an erotic world with the descendant and his follower, and now I'm fighting to stay alive. Living this long, you experience many things, but I never thought such horrific violence would reach me or Momma personally, and if I survive, Malloy will regret not only doing this to my hand, but fully turning me. I'm the rightful heir to the throne of our coven and I will be successful.

Mark my words.

Malloy will watch his queen die a violent death, and his precious sons will witness his.

CHAPTER EIGHT

Maxsimus has been gone for a while, and the roamers have been hunting animals in the woods, giving me what I need to feed as they drain them. I always feel bad to see life leave any species, but it's critical for me to at least keep my levels up until something is decided about my hand. More importantly, Momma is in excruciating pain and although the roamers are helping her with her burns, there's nothing they can do other than soothe her until her body can somewhat heal.

There have been vamps in the past who have been burned, not dusted by the sunlight, but most don't make it because the damage is too great, but my mother is a warrior.

"Momma, I'm sorry."

My voice finally returns, and she looks at me attempting to smile.

"It's not your fault."

"It is my fault. I gave the descendants an offering and I know the truth."

"I know. Malloy made it clear."

"How did he know?"

"I'm not sure."

"We need to make an offering to the descendants so they can heal your burns."

"No. If the descendants help anyone, it will be you."

"They can help us both, Momma. I won't let you suffer."

"I love you."

"I love you too. I promise I'll never go against your wishes again."

"You have always had an adventurous spirit with no fear. I only wanted to protect you from Malloy."

"You didn't fight the punishment he was giving. Why?"

"Because you are my life, and if it means you would be unharmed, I'd do it again."

"I'm honored to be your daughter."

"The honor is mine, my little rainbow."

A roamer brings over fresh linens for my hand, and I realize it's the same female I saw run out of here days ago. As she and Momma redress my wound, I take her in. Even with the mutation, if you look closely you can see she was young when she became a roamer, maybe early twenties like I was, so I close my eyes and imagine what she looked like before and my vibrant imagination does not disappoint. I see a beautiful girl, full of life, and it makes me happy. I've done this many times with Maxsimus, but I try not to because he's handsome just the way he is.

The girl roamer moves closer to me once my new dressing is done, and rests her head on my shoulder, nuzzling my neck. She's showing compassion and love, so I wrap my good arm around her to return the gesture. She's non-verbal, but her actions speak better words than I have ever accomplished.

We're startled when the door swings open, slamming against the wall behind it, and I feel bad yet again when I see who it is. It's another roamer who is verbal, but I've never bothered to remember his name.

"Malloy and the royals are in the woods. We must move."

Sounds like a great plan, but my mom can't move freely in the sunlight.

"What about my momma?"

"She must stay."

"No. I will not leave without her."

"This is an order from Maxsimus."

"You tell Maxsimus we aren't going anywhere until nightfall."

Momma takes my hand. "Go, Amalee, you are too important to stay."

"No, Momma."

"Please go. I will be fine."

"Malloy will kill you. We stay and fight."

"Please go."

"I'm not leaving you. One hand or not, no one will ever hurt you again." I turn to the girl roamer. "Can you stay with her, please?"

She nods and I stand on shaky legs to even my equilibrium, and I'm not quite strong enough, but for my mom I will toughen up. The male roamer blocks the door as I try to pass, and now isn't the time for this.

"We must go together."

"If you're making my mother stay, I'll take my chances out there with Malloy. It's me he wants."

"You've lost too much blood. You will not make it far without replenishment."

"Again, I'll take my chances. Now if you'll excuse me, please?"

He takes a step to the side and before I'm halfway through the door, it's as if my brain turns off and my legs don't know how to function and I'm grateful for the unconsciousness before I hit the floor.

When I open my eyes, it's dark, but I'm in a massive cave. I can hear the waves crashing in the distance.

Maxsimus leans over me, brushing my cheek. "How do you feel?"

"I don't feel any pain. Where's my mom?"

"She's safe. You must rest."

"Are you sure?"

"Yes, you've been through trauma."

"No, are you sure my mom is safe?"

"Yes, I give you my word."

"What about Malloy?"

"He retreated back to the grounds."

"Do you think he's waiting for nightfall?"

"Yes. The coven will take over the woods until they find you."

"Why is he so mad at me?"

"You were never meant to know the truth."

"Then why did you let me give an offering to the descendant?"

"You deserved to know."

"Why didn't you tell me?"

"Another time. You rest."

There's no reasoning with Maxsimus when he doesn't want to speak openly, so I turn my focus to my hand, and I'm eerily spooked by what I see. Malloy cut my four fingers and half of my thumb clean off, and now it almost looks like it never happened.

Almost.

Up the middle from my wrist to where the fingers begin shows no signs of a wound, and I have fingers again. They aren't the ones I had connected to my body and it's a little hard to get a perfect look since the tight bandaging which is being used as a splint is semi opaque, but I have fingers.

"Max, how did they do this?"

"The descendants are powerful beings, and you are strong."

"I wish I was stronger and not allowed my hand to be damaged."

"Do not dwell on it. It is in the past now. What would you prefer to do with Malloy?"

"I'd like to kill him."

"Very well. We will move before sunset."

There's no telling how long it will take for my new hand to heal, so I close my mouth, and get the much needed rest to face Malloy one last time. My hopes are high in dethroning him at the very least, but I know him, and he will not surrender or remain alive without being the king.

It's time to make things right.

CHAPTER NINE

The time has come to make my way back to the woods and face my maker. Well, one of them, anyway.

Maxsimus and his trusty roamers are asleep, so I walk as stealthily as my body will allow and I'm surprised when I get to the entrance of the cave. I'm not on the beach as I thought, but in the woods. There are waves crashing against the side of the cave, which is magical to my eyes, since no water hits the inside, but I can't be mesmerized in a time like this. I need to find Momma before making the journey to Malloy.

Being a vamp heightens our senses, and we're able to see and hear better if it wasn't an issue before being turned. Knowing now that I was born a royal confirms why my senses are out of this world impeccable.

Why didn't he kill me? He chose to unleash the same powers as him, making me an unstoppable force.

Then it hits me like a ton of bricks. Malloy may be in love with Momma, and I think the punishment was because he was rejected by her.

The plot thickens, and I'm glad there is no time to dwell, so I quietly move further into the woods, hoping the enemies I was taught to avoid don't make an appearance. If Malloy can't find me, then he'll stop at nothing to draw me back to the castle grounds, but I need my hand to heal more before I can fight.

I've heard the stories about the deep woods, and I thought it was only to scare us, but this unnerving feeling slowing moving through my body says there is some truth to it all. It's colder than the beach at dawn, which is shocking because the part of the woods the roamers dwell in is typically a comfortable temperature. Same with the castle's grounds.

The eerie sounds remind me of almost every scary movie I've watched with Amina when woods are involved, so I'm not as scared as I should be, until something rushes past, going in circles and I freeze in place because they're moving too fast and it's too dark for me to make out if I'm in danger or not. I don't feel like I should be running in the opposite direction, but just in case, I stay as still as possible, hoping whatever it is, tuckers itself out and leaves me be.

Then it stops about ten feet away and I roll my eyes so hard, it hurts a little. "Max, is that you?"

Maxsimus steps closer with a grin. "You should not be out here alone, Amalee."

"Where's my momma?"

"Safe."

"Why won't you tell me where she is?"

"Because you will expose her location."

"Promise she's okay."

"Have I ever misled you?"

"No, I'm worried about her."

"She is safe and healing. What you should be doing."

"I can't. It's all my fault."

"No, it is not. Malloy is a cruel man who feeds on power and intimidation."

"It's not a mystery. Why didn't you stop him?"

"I love you dearly, Amalee, but there was nothing I could do. I'm sorry."

"Why did he leave when you told him to stop?"

"Come, and I will tell you."

I follow him further into the woods until we reach a familiar sight. The same beautiful rock I gave myself to the descendant on, but we don't go into the water, instead we walk past it and settle into a cave like the one I woke up in.

"Are we safe here?" I ask, sitting next to him.

"Yes. I am terribly sorry for not telling you the truth."

"You don't have to be sorry. Will you tell me every-thing now?"

"Yes." His discomfort speaks volumes. "When I was a boy, I had no family left due to unfortunate circum-stances, and I wandered around asking for food, until Malloy's father took me in. I became a part of their family."

"I knew there was more!"

"Amalee, please."

"Sorry."

"Malloy had jealousy in his heart because I took to things his father taught us. He was unwilling to help provide for the family and it set a divide between us."

"You became brothers?"

"Yes. When we were men, we went our separate ways, and for many years I did not think of him. One evening, I was tending to the cattle, and he ambushed me along with six others."

"You were already turned by then, right?"

"No, it was that night I became what I am now."

"So Malloy turned you?"

"Yes."

"But mutation only happens when the mix of host blood is tainted."

"True. A royal is the only one who has the power to turn a human successfully."

I don't know if I should cry or laugh.

"You're saying Malloy isn't a royal?"

"Yes."

"But he is my father?"

"Yes."

"Please explain to me how a regular vamp bit me and Momma and we didn't mutate."

"Genieva is a royal."

"I don't understand what you're telling me, Max."

"Malloy did not bite you or your mother. It was her."

"Lies."

I can't listen to this nonsense anymore, so I rush out of the cave, to the shoreline and stare at the crashing waves before me.

Maxsimus has woven an unintelligible story into my mind, and I don't know why? He has always been full of happiness and knowledge, but his story simply doesn't make sense. If Momma is a royal, she wouldn't have been burned by the sunlight, and Malloy wouldn't survive it. And how in the world would the two princes have the ability to walk around during the day?

No matter what I believe, I know Maxsimus wouldn't treat me in a malicious way so if what he's saying is true, it's because he was told this.

Back in the cave, I sit next to him, and he looks at me with sadness. "I am sorry."

"If what you're saying is factual, explain how it's possible."

"Malloy made an offering to Cthulhu to reverse the powers within."

"Within whom?"

"He and Genieva. In doing so, your mother's memory was altered, but I do believe she remembers now."

"How did she give birth to me if she was born a royal? Lady vamps can't conceive."

"She is one of a kind, but it is not only you who she birthed."

Forget laughing or crying. Now I don't know if I should throw up or pass out.

Cthulhu is a powerful being and if Malloy presented the right offering, there's no way the sea god would have turned him away. But one thing I do know as a fact is if a spell was cast, it can be undone, and it's exactly what I'll do to defeat Malloy and return Momma to her rightful state.

There are a few more things I need to know before I make my way back to the ocean. "Who did she birth, Max?"

"Jasper and Holden."

His words do not surprise me in the slightest, and I need to be careful because the princes are strong and will protect their father by any means necessary. Unless I can convince them of Malloy's lies; then there is a chance to end this peacefully.

If not, the coven will embark on what the humans know as a civil war.

CHAPTER TEN

Sleeping in the cave with Maxsimus is my new favorite thing. His overprotectiveness is incredible, and I love it. Of course, I'm worried about Momma and making another offering to the descendants, but the only way to keep my mind steady is enjoying being in his arms. Learning the truth still hasn't sunk in so to speak, but I trust Max and I know he hates Malloy as much as I do, so we'll fight together.

Staring at him while he's in a deep sleep sends flutters of weird feelings through my body, and I'm certain it means I'm in love. Any vamp who lives on the castle grounds is forbidden to procreate with the roamers, but seeing as how things have drastically changed, I don't give a damn, no matter what the outcome is. Now to convince Maxsimus I'm his true love is the task I'm not sure I can accomplish.

Normally when I make my attempts to wake him up, I use my backside to press against him, but since we're facing each other, I take it as the perfect opportunity to kiss him. I've dreamt of the day our lips would meet for the first time, and a part of me is screaming for me not to do it because it may anger him, and if it goes in that direction I'll blame it on the events caused by Malloy.

Pushing the hesitation and fear aside, I lift my head without disturbing him, pressing my lips gently to his. This causes him to stir, opening his eyes, so I retreat like a child and rest my head back to where it lied before.

"Amalee, look at me."

His voice is tender, and it may be due to being woken up abruptly, but I do as he asks, looking him into his eyes.

"I'm sorry."

"No apologies necessary."

"So, you're okay with it?"

"Have you ever questioned my reasoning for not pursuing you?"

"Of course, but I thought it was because we were forbidden to even talk to each other."

"A rule set forth by an empty-headed fool."

"Then what was the reason?"

"You are a royal and you cannot take a lover who is not handsome in appearance."

Oh, my beatless heart. I never thought in a millennia Maxsimus would be one to have insecurities over the way he looks. There is a unique attractiveness to him, and along with his beautiful, intelligent mind, there is no way anyone could resist his charm.

Using my good hand, I touch his ice cold cheek and smile. "Royal or not, I know we're meant to be together and anyone who scoffs at us or you will not be tolerated."

"A public dusting?"

"Yes, and I won't feel any shame in doing it. I know it wouldn't make me any better than Malloy, but I am his offspring."

"No. You are the daughter of Genieva and will rule the coven fairly."

"I'm not ready to rule the coven."

"You will when your time comes."

"Thank you, Max."

The most handsome thing about Maxsimus is his smile, and it melts my heart whenever I see it, but when he leans forward, pressing his lips to mine, my mind explodes into a million bright pieces like a firework, and if I weren't a member of the undead, I could safely say I'm in Heaven, staring at Jesus Christ himself in all of his magnificent glory. But of course, Max isn't the type to "half-ass" anything, so I'm on another level when he rolls on top of me and, like magic, effortlessly guides himself inside me.

Is there a place higher than Heaven?

I'm sure if we can walk around being vamps anything is possible, and I never want this to end.

"Take me away, Amalee," he whispers into my ear as he makes the sweetest love to me.

I've never had this before and I'm joyous because if someone else had done what Maxsimus is doing to me now, I would have sold my soul to the actual Devil to keep them in my life. Actually, no one can convince me anyone prior could have because it was meant to happen with Max, even though it's taken nearly eighty years.

Better late than never, and one or both of us may not live through the evening, but at least I can take this beautiful memory to wherever we go once we leave.

I feel weightless as he picks up the speed of his thrusts, but in no way is it uncontrolled, and I always knew he'd be the best lover. It helps that we care for each other, and I'm confident it's making this experience astronomically better.

Then the best thing all women wish for when engaging in sexual acts is the moment your body lights on fire, you tense, and you're overtaken by the natural feeling of true pleasure. I've had orgasms before and they were good, but this is great and I hope he understands if we are able to stop Malloy, he will do this to me every moment we're alone.

Once Maxsimus's body relaxes, I kiss him and the

fluttering in my body doesn't retreat. In fact, it's more intense when he pulls back a little, looking into my eyes.

"I love you, Max."

"I love you too."

"Promise you won't abandon me?"

"Only if you promise to never abandon me."

"It isn't an option."

"Will you be my bride?"

"Yes."

"We must offer a truce to Malloy until you can fight."

"You think that's best?"

"Yes."

"Okay, but once I'm healed, we kill him."

"It will be what you younglings call a blindside."

A giggle escapes, pushing his soft penis out. "So, you do pay attention."

"I never miss a word you say, Amalee."

"I never miss a word you say either."

Another kiss and I'm back in his arms, resting my body, but my mind is working every scenario possible to defeat our imposter king. Malloy doesn't know I have all of the answers, and he'll believe he's in full control after we ask for a truce, which is perfection for us. It will give us the time we need to prepare our army for battle and a blindside is exactly what the coven needs.

The time has come to reveal my new hand, and I'm scared because for the past week Maxsimus has been extremely anxious, pacing around his dwelling without sleeping more than an hour at a time. The evening after we made love, he sent two roamers to the castle grounds with written word of the truce and they haven't returned, so it means one thing. Malloy has accepted, but is making it clear it's not for long.

It's been quiet over the week, and Momma was brought back a few days ago and she's healed back to normal. She's been ranting and raving about the descendant and his "creature" hood, and all I could do is smile because I know how she feels. Of course, I hold the grin to a minimum if Max is looking at me, but he's no fool and knows their talent with women.

After the sun has set, the roamers are in their designated places to protect the woods from the coven, and we make our way to the beach to meet with the descendant to unveil my hand. I was told I needed to be with him just in case something is wrong, and he can take action right away, and since I made a lasting impression on him, there will be no further offerings. Maxsimus told me not to abuse the privilege and I'm taking the advice, promising only to use it if absolutely necessary.

"Your spirits are high this evening, Amalee," Max says, holding my good hand a little tighter.

"I'm nervous about what I'll see, but there hasn't been a vamp sighting in eight days."

"We will not wait much longer."

"Can you lighten up until that time comes? It's hard to sleep when you aren't."

"Yes."

Now our conversation is over and after we defeat Malloy, we'll have to talk about how he shuts down on me midway through important things. I give him the benefit of the doubt because he's been alone for so long with the other roamers and they aren't much for talking, but I have to express how I feel, or I'll lose my mind.

Before we reach the beach, I pull Maxsimus close to me and look up at him. "We may need to keep Momma away from the descendant."

His gorgeous grin melts me. "I understand. Phineas has taken a liking to her."

"Which one is he again?"

"The one you give ugly looks to all of the time."

Ah, the roamer who is Max's second in command. The same one who tried stopping me from going out into the woods alone after my fingers were dismembered. I feel terrible for never remembering his name, but knowing he has a crush on Momma, I'll never forget again.

The roamers lead us to the beach, separating when we get to the shoreline, leaving me with Maxsimus and Momma, and I somewhat wish I hadn't begged her to come along instead of staying with Phineas because there are tears in her eyes, and I don't want to cry tonight.

She takes my face into her hands and kisses my nose. "Everything will be okay, little rainbow."

"I know, Momma. You should stay here on land."

Maxsimus clears his throat, and he gives me a strange look when I turn to him, and it's not my brightest moment, but if I ask the descendant to reverse the spell, she has to be with me.

I focus back on her. "I don't know if I can handle seeing my hand."

"I will be at your side, and I want you to remember this does not take away from your beauty."

"Thank you, Momma."

The saying is *there's no time like the present*, so we follow Maxsimus to a small boat, and after we're in, he pushes it until the bottom release from the shore floor, and I'm so glad he's here to row us out because it's a long way to the rock where we're meeting the descendant. Luckily, my roamer has no shortage of physical strength, and the trip isn't as long as I anticipated, but there is one problem and Momma sees it too.

"Amalee cannot climb with one hand, Maxsimus."

As if on cue, we're hit with a massive wave, knocking the three of us out of the boat, and when I come above water, the descendant is at the rock, so I wait my turn as he lifts Momma and let out a small giggle when Maxsimus refuses, climbing up himself.

The descendant holds out his arm and I climb on. "Thank you."

"This is my finest work."

"I trust you didn't do anything silly. Cthulhu cast a spell for Malloy. Are you aware?"

"Yes."

"With the proper offering, can you reverse it?"

"Yes. No offering is required at this time."

"You like me a little, don't you?"

"Our time is appreciated," he says into my head, lifting me onto the rock.

What?

Sea creatures use tongue twisters in the same way the older vamps do and it's confusing, but there's no time to ponder. I need to see my hand.

Momma and Maxsimus sit on either side of me, and

I hold out my hand to the descendant and he uses a face tentacle to somehow cut the wrapping without harming me and all I can mumble out when I see my new fingers is *oh*. My thumb is as it was before, but my four fingers are now small tentacles. I can move them like I normally would with human appendages, and I'll admit it's interesting, but I can't be upset since the descendant sounded proud of his work, but again. I have no idea how these will give me a functioning hand.

I look up into the eyes of the sea royal, which I shouldn't, but I have nothing to lose at this point.

"Thank you. One question. How do I use these things?"

He moves his head closer. *"You now have a natural weapon. When in fear or sense an enemy, the suckers will produce spines or quills and open to attack your prey."*

"That's cool."

"Word of caution, Amalee. You must touch the flesh of your prey for the spines to release."

"Still cool."

"They will only produce when you are in distress."

"Got it. What happens once they're released?"

"Death."

"I thank you again. Can we do the other thing now?"

"Yes."

Momma leans over close to my ear. "What are we doing now?"

"You'll see."

The three of us sit, watching the descendant and he's making strange noises, but once others just like him emerge from the water, I realize they'll be reversing the spell as one. Then the noises stop, and Momma is lifted into the descendant's arm and chanting begins. It's not English or any language I can say I've heard before, so it must be the Old Ones' language, but she doesn't seem scared, so I lean against Maxsimus, and we wait for it to end.

When the chanting stops, Momma is placed back on the rock next to me and I'm confused. Mister sea royal has some explaining to do.

"It is complete."

"Nothing happened."

"It wasn't meant for your comprehension."

And with that, he disappears under the water and now I have to explain to my mom what the chanting was supposed to be for.

CHAPTER TWELVE

The only way off of the rock is to jump, so I take a running start, leaping into the water. Thankfully our boat didn't end up too far away, and when we're back on land, the roamers come over to inspect my new fingers. Most of them are expressionless, but they are in fact interested and I don't blame them because I am too, and I can't wait to test the new weapons.

Phineas rushes over to Mama, asking if she's unharmed, and I see the twinkle in her eye, but their perfect moment is ruined when we hear a girl's screams getting closer and I run as fast as I can because I know my best friend's voice, and when two non-verbal roamers appear, holding Amina's arms, I stop.

"Let her go."

They do as I say, and she runs to me, wrapping her arms around me. "Amalee, they're coming right now!"

"Malloy?"

"Most of the coven and the royal guards, too."

"Not the princes?"

"They refused."

"Interesting."

She tries to take my hands, and I pull my left one away, holding it up. "Amalee, you have a sea squid on your hand."

"A gift from the descendants."

"O-kay…"

My best friend is in a state of shock, so I motion for Momma to console her, and when my future stands next to me, I feel sheer comfort as we hear the voices off in the distance.

"Do you hear them, Amalee?"

"I think I have an idea."

"Go on."

"We need to draw them back to the grounds and hold them there until sunrise."

"Why? They will have ample time to get cover."

"I know the lighthouse and dungeon vamps, and once they hear the truth, they will turn on Malloy."

"You are certain of this?"

"Yes, and I know because they love Momma."

"We will walk the shoreline to avoid detection."

"Thank you for listening to me."

He touches my cheek gently. "You are mine, and respect will never be lost."

Phineas announces the proximity of the coven, and after Maxsimus gives clear, direct orders, we make our way to the beach, and the noises from the woods are clearer with the vamps talking way too loudly and I'm almost hoping a sneak attack isn't a part of the fake king's plan.

What a yuppie.

Before I let out an inappropriate giggle, I see a mass of bodies emerge from the woods' edge and the roamers don't hesitate to surround us, but I step in front of them when I realize they're all dungeon vamps, and the second they see me, an elder male stops in front of me, giving me a hug.

"I am sorry to hear what he did to you and Genieva."

I hold up my hand with a smile. "I'm fine, and Momma is all healed. Will you fight with us?"

"Yes. Malloy has dusted anyone who refused to join him in ending your life."

"How many?"

"Nearly a quarter of the coven. Prince Holden begged the rest of us to follow suit to keep our lives."

"I'm glad you did. This is what you need to do. Go to Malloy and tell him we're headed back to the grounds."

"Amalee, they will have the upper hand."

"It's okay. I'll explain once we're all there."

He nods and, when the group disappears back into the woods, the rest of us move faster to guarantee we arrive before Malloy and those who are truly following their "king". At this pace it cuts the journey time in half, and we're all weary when we reach the grounds and see no one wandering about. It's clear Malloy is panicked and thinks taking every able-bodied vamp will serve him some justice.

"They are approaching." Maxsimus says, looking toward the woods.

"It's time for the climax."

"Whose climax?"

"Ours. I don't mean an orgasm, Max."

"I wasn't insinuating you were."

"You're too much. Now isn't the time."

"There is always time."

"Never mind that. What do we do?"

"You kill Malloy."

The first to reach the grounds are the group of dungeon vamps we saw, and they immediately run behind us , and when Malloy takes his first step out of the woods, he yells for them to get back in line, and I love seeing his frustration when they don't comply.

Now it's time to give him what he deserves for trying to kill my momma.

"I see you sold your body once again, Amalee." He says, pointing to my new hand.

"I didn't sell anything, Malloy, but it makes me wonder what length you went to betray my mother."

"What?"

I push past him to face the rest of the coven who is

standing at the wood line. "Malloy is no royal. He's a mere human, who craves what is not rightfully his."

"Stupid girl. When will you learn to keep your rambles to yourself?"

"When you're dead."

My senses fail me, and Malloy's slap is irritating, but if it weren't for Maxsimus taking charge, attacking his former friend, I'd most likely would have been hit again, but the squabble doesn't last long as Jasper and Holden separate them. I'm pulled aggressively by my arm, startling me, and my hand with the newly constructed fingers takes over. It isn't until I see who it is that I'm not sad to have grabbed their throat.

It's Rubia and I feel the most splendid tickle throughout my fingers, so I squeeze a little tighter until a small rush escapes each digit, then her eyes go wide, and any color left on her skin is drained and I release her to crumple onto the hard cobblestones at my feet.

"You bitch. What did you do to her?" Malloy shouts, rushing to his now deceased wife.

I feel no guilt or fear until I look toward Maxsimus, but lock eyes with Holden on the way.

"You killed my mother."

"Wait." Taking a deep breath, I prepare to raise my voice for everyone to hear. "Malloy is not our king. He's an imposter who gave an offering to Cthulhu to claim the gifts of a royal."

Holden looks quizzically at Jasper, then back to me. "You're lying to justify your behavior."

"It's the truth, and Rubia was not your mother. However, you are true royals."

"Prove it."

"Malloy is the host that mutates the turning vamps. Max, tell them."

"She speaks the truth. Malloy is the host, and I confirm that I am the first mutation."

What? Things have become a lot more interesting and Maxsimus is a lot older than I thought. By the stories told within the vampire world, the first mutation happened over five centuries ago and within a year's span, the first was joined by hundreds, maybe thousands of who we now call roamers.

Maxsimus has a lot of talking to do once this is done.

While the coven takes in what's been said, the two princes look to our father for answers, but Malloy is staring at me with the most malicious expression. I think the term is, *if looks could kill I'd be dead.* Good thing it's not possible, but my guard is high because the next thing I will say should solidify the separation of our coven. Those who will follow Momma, and the ones who will remain loyal to Malloy.

"Everyone, there's more. Malloy gave an offering to Cthulhu himself to gain the royal gift of day walking. A spell was cast and, upon completion, the royal was stripped of their power and memory."

Jasper turns his head slowly in bewilderment. "Who's the royal?"

"Our mother."

Momma isn't one to enjoy being the center of attention, but as everyone turns to her, she lifts her head high and stands next to me. "My memory was returned through Amalee's gift in the womb. I am the heir to the coven of Dartualo."

I jerk my head so fast it hurts, and I'm not sure if I'm more surprised that she's had her memory my entire life or that she is among the original coven. But as each vamp, including the roamers, kneel with bowed heads, my night just keeps getting better and better.

Unfortunately, we've been dilly dallying for far too long and it's almost sunrise, so Mama instructs everyone to return to their quarters, and once they're safe, Malloy laughs, clapping his disgusting hands.

"Quite the theatrics. We all know the truth and filling my coven with blasphemous claims will only result in death."

"You're right. There will be a death carried out." I step forward the same way he did the day he tried to kill Momma. "Sunrise is upon us, Malloy."

"I do not fear the sun, my darling."

"And you never will because this is your last. Now is the time to tell your sons the truth."

"The sun will reveal the truth." He leans in, pressing his lips to my ear. "The spell is irreversible. I will spare your mother this time. Get her inside."

Malloy stands straight with a demented smile of victory across his mouth, so I match it. "As you said, the sun will reveal the truth. I have one question."

"What is it?"

"How did the roamers become day walkers?"

"Maxsimus, you are a worthier storyteller than I," he says, looking at his former friend.

"Before the second turning, unleashing the royal gift's purity, if bitten by a common vampire, creates the mutation, but the gift to walk in the sunlight remains."

"So roamers are birthed royals?"

"Yes."

"What coven are you from?"

"Coven of Crotaun."

The original coven of Dartualo saw it fit to have more than one to keep vampires safe against enemies and the promising younger vamps started Crotaun. It seems as though there will be many days ahead full of magnificent stories because Malloy is right. Maxsimus is a tremendous storyteller.

As much as I would love to ask more questions, the sky begins to wake up and Malloy stands defiantly with the same smile on his face, but just in the case the descendants didn't reverse the spell, I take Momma's hand and wait for the first ray from the sun to shine through the clouds.

No matter if you're among the living or undead, anxiety is real and I'm feeling it more than ever, then it happens and we're all looking from Malloy to Momma to see who is dusted, and it's possible the sun is still half-asleep because nothing is happening to either of them.

"What's going on?" I ask loudly to no one in particular.

Everyone slowly shakes their heads, then like a gift from Cthulhu, the clouds break and the sun beams down upon us and Momma takes me into her arms as we watch Malloy's skin begin to burn, but he's a stubborn old goat. Instead of howling in pain, he attempts to run for cover, only for the roamers to restrain him, and we watch as he burns at a rapid speed, turning to dust, leaving the clothing, shield, and weapons in a pile on the ground. To my greatest sight, Rubia's body also dusts, and I wish them well wherever they end up in the universe.

Momma takes my face into her hands and kisses my nose. "You did it, my little rainbow."

"Why didn't you tell me?"

"To protect you. To protect all three of you. Holden tasting your blood caused a stir within Malloy."

I look at Holden and he shrugs, realizing by him telling our father about my blood is what caused the spiraling of events. He isn't at fault since we didn't know, but we know now, although it's only a fraction, and I can't wait to hear it all.

Now that that's out of the way, it's instantly awkward, so I break from Momma's hold and grab Maxsimus' hand, pulling him into the woods far enough to where we're out of sight but we can see what's going on.

"Are you not satisfied, Amalee?"

"I am, but they need to talk, and I can't assume they'll be nice."

"Jasper knew."

The same abrupt jerking of my neck in surprise happens. "He did? Why didn't you tell me?"

"As Genieva said. To protect you."

"He's a good actor, and you have a lot of explaining to do."

"Yes. Are you willing to hear it?"

"You know how much I love your stories. So, what is your title?"

"Duke."

"Ah, a peasant among the princess."

A genuine laugh leaves his body, making me smile because I've never heard Maxsimus do it quite like this, but I'm glad he always understands my humor.

We watch Momma with the princes and before long, they're hugging and I'm so happy to see her joy. Sure, I didn't know I wasn't her only child, and I have so many things I need clarification on, but for now, I won't press it until she's ready to share. Malloy is gone, so we have all the time in the world to get answers. In the meantime, I have my roamer king to keep me occupied and while we hold each other after making love, my ears better be filled with stories of the past.

"I smell your lust."

"What does that mean?"

"You are yearning for my touch, Amalee."

"You can smell that?"

"Yes."

"Could you smell it before the cave?"

"Yes."

"Oh. Then you knew how I truly felt about you."

"Yes."

"You are full of many words, Max."

"I have a natural talent."

Finally, a giggle can escape when it's not the wrong time, and after a gorgeous grin from Maxsimus, he pulls me back onto the grounds to see what's going on with Momma and the princes. They aren't saying anything, but no one is trying to kill the other, so I think it's safe to say everything is going well.

Momma looks at us with a smile. "There you two are. We are going up to the castle to sort things out before the coven awakes. And, Amalee, you can pick your room."

"Actually, with your permission, I'd like to stay wherever Max is."

"I was hoping you both would occupy the castle."

Maxsimus lets go of my hand. "I appreciate the offer, my lady, but I will remain in the woods."

"As you wish. You and the roamers are always welcome anywhere on the grounds."

"Thank you."

We watch the three of them walk away and when they disappear into the castle, I turn to my future. "Stay in the woods?"

"It is my home."

"Now it's my home too."

"Our home is wherever we are together."

"I like that. Let's go home."

He retakes my hand, and we walk leisurely back into the woods toward our dwelling, and there's an odd feeling in the air.

"What is it, Amalee?"

"Does it seem like everything happened so fast?"

"It did."

"Malloy didn't put up a fight."

"He was anticipating a victory."

"Serves him right. Do you think Momma will be okay with the princes?"

"Yes."

"So, what now?"

"Anything we desire."

"I desire a lot of you."

"And I you."

A quick smirk from Maxsimus and we enjoy our walk filled with lighthearted conversation about the newest events, and I still can't believe how fast and easy it was to get rid of Malloy. If I had known this sooner, I would have acted on it, but as Momma always says *things happen accordingly and not when you expect,* and I will always love her wisdom. With her claiming the coven, things are as bright as they can be for all of us, especially me and Maxsimus, and I hope the fluttering in my belly when he's near never goes away.

Now we start our new adventure together and maybe one day I can convince him to go with me to the mainland.

ACKNOWLEDGMENTS

A special thanks to Rachel with Blue Raven Book Covers for the cover art and formatting of this collection.

You can find her complete portfolio at blueraven bookcovers.wordpress.com.